Chloe

Book Four of
The Siblings O'Rifcan Series

By Katharine E. Hamilton

ISBN-13: 978-0-578-45298-2

Chloe

www.katharinehamilton.com

Cover Design by Kerry Prater.

Dedicated to my family.

Hamilton and O'Neal

I love that we have a large and loving group of people we can call family.

We may be spread out all over the country, but I'm thankful for each and every one of you.

Acknowledgments

Brad for being patient on my late-night writing sessions... I promise to dim the screen better.

My family. They are on this journey with me and have supported me every step of the way.

Sherrill Crisp, with Crisp Floral Design, for insight into a florist's world. Though much of what I gleaned from our conversations will carry over into the next book, Sherrill helped me define Chloe and Chloe's work ethic. Thanks, Sherrill!!!

My alpha and beta readers. Patience is definitely their virtue.

Thanks to my editor, Lauren Hanson. She's quick to straighten out my quirks and mistakes. And yet another patient person that tolerates me.

And thanks to my readers. I love meeting you. I love hearing from you. And I love writing for you. You guys are awesome.

« CHAPTER ONE »

"There's an order on the counter, love. Be a dear and grab it on your way out." Chloe O'Rifcan swiftly grabbed the two dishes, scanning the ticket on her way out of the kitchen doors and towards the awaiting table. She slid the plates in front of the hungry patrons and then waved through the small window separating the dining hall and the kitchen to a pleased Doireann McCarthy. Chloe had been lending an extra set of hands to Mrs. McCarthy while her son, Conor, had been helping with various carpentry projects for her siblings. The poor guy worked himself to the bone, and his main job— helping his mother with the family restaurant— had been placed on the back burner as the O'Rifcan family continued to monopolize his time.

Chloe untied her apron and placed it on the hook by the door as she hurried up the sidewalk to her own shop. Opening the door, she smiled as her sister, Layla, walked a customer around her own half of the store showcasing her various scented candles. Layla offered a brief wave in greeting before returning to her customer. Chloe hopped on the worn stool behind her counter and flipped open her schedule. She had two flower arrangements that needed to be created by end of day. *Easy enough*, she thought, as she set about stalking her coolers for the right shades of colors and complimentary stems.

She adored flowers. Always had. Even as a girl, she could be found at her grandparents' house on the hill at Angel's Gap, sitting in the tall grass, weaving flower crowns and talking to the fairies. Now her brother, Claron, occupied the house at the Gap, and she often visited and sat on that very hill to soak in the scenery, revive her creative mindset, and perhaps still talk to a fairy or two. Flowers kept her balanced. She always felt at home amongst the petals and scents. She sniffed the rich aroma of the lilacs in her hand and immediately felt at ease. Relaxed, she walked her shelves to find the perfect vase. The phone at the counter rang, and she walked over quickly so Layla's conversation with her customer would not be interrupted by incessant ringing.

"Chloe's Flowers," she greeted.

"Chloe, it's Delaney." Always one to get straight down to business, Layla's boyfriend continued without interruption from Chloe. "I need a favor, if possible."

"Of course. All you need's to ask, you know that."

"Well, I'm planning a special dinner tonight for Layla. I wondered, if you are to be around her today, whether you might deliver her a rose for me. A single rose."

"Aye, I can do that. Any specific time?"

"Preferably as close to five as possible. I'm to pick her up at six."

"I can mange that for you." She penciled a reminder on her schedule for the day. "Any specific color?"

"Red. She likes the bold."

"That she does." Chloe smiled into the phone, pleased that Delaney knew her sister so well. "Consider it done."

"Thank you. Just shoot me a text on how much I owe you and I'll send payment."

"Of course. Thanks, D—" She trailed off so as not to let Layla hear.

"She's there, isn't she?" Delaney asked.

"Yes."

He chuckled. "Thanks for the discretion, Chloe. Talk soon."

Placing the phone back in its cradle, Chloe glanced over at her sister and smiled. Layla, her beautiful brown hair draped over her shoulders and blue eyes sparkling as she laughed with her patron, had found love in the most unlikely of men. Delaney Hawkins was a man of business, and he took everything in his life seriously... even her sister. But somehow, Layla softened him, and he in turn challenged her sister. It was meant. Sighing with a wistful heart, Chloe went back to her shelves.

Life in Castlebrook had changed over the last year. Claron found love with the brilliant and beautiful Rhea Connors from Maryland. Riley had been ensnared by the audacious Heidi Rustler from Texas. And Layla had snagged her own love right out from under the other two women's noses in the form of their boss, Delaney Hawkins. Love was in the air it seemed, and though Chloe was happy for her siblings— tremendously happy— she also felt a longing in her own heart for the same thing to happen to her. Castlebrook was a small village, and she knew it might take some time for her to find her own love since she rarely traveled outside of the town. But deep down, Chloe felt her love was here in Castlebrook. She'd always felt deeply rooted to the village, and she had no desire to leave, even for love. So she'd made her peace with fate, and should fate decide to bring her a love here to Castlebrook, Chloe would patiently await the day. And if fate decided not to... well, Chloe hadn't figured out her plan for that yet. Either way, Castlebrook was her home and her heart belonged to the prettiest village in County Clare. She plucked a vase off the top shelf and walked it back to the counter. She then went back to her coolers. The purple lilacs needed a complimentary yellow flower, she decided, so she began her method of pairing the right shapes, textures, colors, and scents until the perfect match was found.

∞

Conor McCarthy hoisted the massive oak plank onto the saw table. He brushed a hand over the smooth surface, his palm detecting the areas he'd need to sand down even further. Claron O'Rifcan had commissioned him to help with his dream house renovation, and Conor would do his best to provide his best friend with a table that he and his soon-to-be wife— and should the fates allow it, many children— would share for a lifetime. Family meals were important to the O'Rifcan family. They gathered every evening at Sidna's B&B just for the purpose of sharing dinner together as a family. Those that could make it, anyway. Conor had been granted the privilege of eating at that very table many times over the years, and he wanted to capture that same feel for Clary's table. He and Rhea deserved the best of his abilities. He swiped a hand over his sweaty brow and glanced at his watch. He'd been working all morning and though he'd felt his stomach protesting over an hour ago, he finally realized it was well past lunch time, and he needed to refuel himself in order to finish what he'd planned for the day. He also needed to run by his mam's restaurant and make sure she did not need him for the evening rush later.

He walked over to the sink and washed his hands, splashing the cool water over his face as well. Saw dust clung to every inch of him, and though he didn't mind, he knew his mammy would. He stepped from the dusty shop, the small space nestled between O'Malley's Market and the store's extra storage space. Tom O'Malley rented the small storefront to Conor at a reasonable price which worked out perfectly, in Conor's mind. With all the work he'd been doing, he needed a space larger than his back porch, and Tom needed to fill the spot. It worked well for both of them, and those were always the best business deals to make.

He squinted at the sunshine and tilted his face up to absorb as much of it as he could while outside before heading towards Sidna's B&B and adjacent café to find some lunch. His mother and

Sidna O'Rifcan had been friends long before either of them had children, and both women found their love in feeding people. If he didn't eat his mother's cooking, he was bound to be eating Sidna's, and that was just what he was craving for the day.

He spotted Chloe across the street, slipping out of her shop carrying a large bouquet of flowers. The O'Rifcan sister never slowed down, always working on something. Whether it be her flowers or at their mother's restaurants. She'd been an asset to his mam over the last several months as his work load increased. She caught sight of him and offered a friendly wave and smile as she crossed the street towards him.

"I know those cannot be for me."

She laughed. "I'm afraid not. I be headed to O'Malley's. Seems me brother Tommy wishes to dote upon Denise today."

"Ah. It be a mile marker for them, I believe. Heard Tommy mention it at Murphy's the other night."

"Already?" Her brows rose. "Seems I can't keep up. My siblings are falling in love too fast these days."

He chuckled. "Aye, seems the O'Rifcan clan has pleased the fairies this year."

"It would seem."

He caught a brief look of disappointment that washed over her face and was surprised to see Chloe O'Rifcan with even a resemblance of a frown. "I was just headed to your mam's for some fish and chips. I'll wait if you want to grab a bite."

"That'd be great." She hurried into the market and within less than a minute was back on the footpath. "I've been creating two pieces today, that just be my first." She pointed towards O'Malley's. "The second is a bit of a beast. Figured I best get away before I zone out for the rest of the day."

"Then 'tis about time for ye to grab a meal."

"Exactly. So, how's the table coming along?"

"Almost as smooth as I'd like it to be. A bit of work left on the tabletop, then I can focus on the legs. I wish to do some carving there, but not sure yet what."

"I noticed Layla's stools were missing from the store. Did she send them back to you?"

"No. That be my doing. I confiscated them. Wish to do better carvings. Clean them up a bit. I rushed them so she'd have them at her grand opening, but if they are to last and be special, they need a bit more attention. She was kind enough to let me take them for a bit longer."

"They were beautiful, Conor. I don't see the need to touch them up. Ye're just adding more work to your already busy schedule."

"Aye, there is that. But they be for Layla. They have to be beauties, aye?" He winked at her as she rolled her eyes. "Come. Let's grab a table. Ah—" His eyes danced as he walked towards a table where Claron sat with Rhea. "If it not be two of my favorite people." He greeted them with a smile and invited himself to the table. Chloe slid into the chair next to Rhea.

"Talking business, I see," Conor teased, as he eyed the wedding magazines strung about the table.

"Did you come to rescue me?" Claron asked.

Rhea punched his shoulder and he grabbed her fist and kissed it. "Only kidding, love."

"You better be." She sighed. "I was an idiot to think I could have an entire wedding planned in only two months."

Conor's eyes widened. "Two months, she says?" He looked to Claron. "That be barely a blink of an eye."

"Because," Rhea began, her smile softening as she looked at Claron. "I don't want a winter wedding and next spring just seems too far away. So, September it is."

"It'll be grand," Chloe encouraged. "Though we do need to settle upon some flowers. I'll need to place that order rather quickly."

"Yes, I have a list." Rhea filtered through a notebook, tore a page out, and then handed it to Chloe. "Doable?" she asked.

Chloe nodded. "Aye, but some of these may be a bit expensive, as they're not in their season. But I'll see what I can find and then we can schedule our consultation for when your mam is here."

"That's fine." Rhea waved away her concerns. "My mom flies in next week and will be staying here for the next couple of months to help me. Poor Dad." She shook her head but grinned. "He'll be lost without her, but I desperately need her here."

"Oh, Paul Conners is a good man," Chloe added. "He'll make such a sacrifice for his darling Rhea."

Rhea grinned. "Yep. I don't know who's more in love with Claron, me or my dad." She laughed as she stared into the O'Rifcan brother's green eyes, a silent moment holding between them.

"That'd be hard competition," Conor teased. "Though I have to say, Clary is quite dreamy."

Chloe smirked as Claron's face flushed.

"Alright you two." Claron squeezed Rhea's hand under the table. "What are you two doing here?"

"Eating," they replied in unison.

"Found this fellow coppertop delivering flowers to Denise O'Malley and I was taking a break from your dining table project. Neither of us had eaten. Just made sense."

"You two work too hard." Rhea tucked her hair behind her ear as she gathered up her magazines and stacked them neatly to the side. Emily, an O'Rifcan niece, placed Claron and Rhea's food before them.

"Two fish and chips, Em," Chloe told her. The girl gave a brief nod and walked away.

Conor relaxed his hands on the table and Chloe gasped. "Conor McCarthy!" she scolded, reaching for his right hand. "'Tis a crime to treat your hands so badly." She pointed at several scrapes and fresh blisters that covered his knuckles and palms. She released her grip and tsked her tongue. "I'll have Layla give you a balm."

Embarrassed, Conor tucked his hands in his lap. He caught Rhea's amused grin. "And where you plannin' on taking the lass for the honeymoon, Clary?" Conor wriggled his eyebrows as Rhea laughed.

"That's still to be decided upon," Claron answered. "We can't quite sort it out. I want to take Rhea somewhere exotic, but she'd just like to tour Ireland."

"A beach would be fun," Chloe echoed her brother's sentiments.

"But I have yet to see all of Ireland," Rhea explained.

"Well, you have your whole life for that now, don't you?" Conor asked her.

"I suppose you're right." Rhea looked to Claron. "I don't care where I go with this man. Anywhere with him will be amazing."

"Awe, and just like that they be lost again." Conor waved his hand towards his friends as they lovingly gazed at one another.

"'Tis going to be a long two months," Chloe muttered to him. Conor burst into a hearty laugh that broke through Rhea and Claron's trance.

"What was that?" Claron asked.

"Nothing." Chloe and Conor exchanged a grin.

"Oh, Conor, I have been meaning to ask you something," Claron began. "Rhea and I have been sorting through our wedding party, and I was wondering if you'd be one of my best mates."

"Men," Rhea corrected.

"Men." Claron continued. "Riley be one and I'd like you to be as well."

Conor paused in putting a chip into his mouth. "You want me as a best man?" he asked again.

"Aye." Claron nodded in confirmation. "You and Riley are me best friends."

"And I have two maids of honor," Rhea added by way of an explanation. "Heidi and Chloe."

"What of Layla?"

"She has designated herself— and I am not upset about it— as the official wedding planner, so she will stand as a bridesmaid, but she feels she will be much too busy helping plan the wedding and making sure it runs smoothly," Rhea replied.

"Ah." Conor leaned back in his chair, crossing his arms over his robust chest. "You sure you don't want Murphy?" he asked.

Claron's eyes grew serious. "I'm asking you, Conor. If I wanted Murphy, I'd be asking Murphy. If you don't want to be, I understand. Just wanted to have you up there with me. On the biggest day of me life," he added for good measure. He waited for Conor's response.

"I'd be glad to do it. Honored." Conor's face broke into a large grin as he pumped Claron's hand and slapped him on the back. "Guess I'll be escortin' this gingernut here, hm?" He elbowed Chloe and she gently laid her fish back onto her plate. "Or Heidi."

"I doubt Riley O'Rifcan would ever give up his lass, even for just a minute," Conor joked.

"Well, it was my plan to have you two walk down together," Rhea told them. "Plus, you both have red hair, and will complement one another."

Claron rolled his eyes. "Really?"

"I'm very into details," Rhea told him.

"Oh, I know, love. I know." He chuckled as Rhea waved away his comment. "Now we have all of our wedding party on board. Yay!" She smiled and squeezed both Conor and Chloe's hands. "And Conor, know tearing up the cottage until after the wedding. No matter how hard Claron and Riley try to convince you. I don't want it to be in disarray for the wedding."

"Got it, lass."

Rhea stood, grabbing her magazines. "I better head back to Limerick. Delaney's been extremely lenient with me the last few days, but I don't want to push it." She kissed Claron on the lips as she dug in her purse for her keys. "See you guys later."

They waved as she hurried towards her car and pulled away from the footpath.

"Got yourself a real gem there, Clary." Conor rubbed his napkin over his mouth and beard before standing. "Chloe, thanks for eating with me. Work is calling me back to it."

"Go see Layla about those hands," Chloe reminded him.

He nodded as he shook Claron's hand one more time. "Aye, I'll do that. Clary, see you around." He tossed a few extra bills on the table for Emily, more than was necessary, and followed the footpath back to his shop. Best man. Clary had asked him be a best man at his wedding. Pride swelled in his chest. Yes, Claron was one of his oldest friends, but to be asked to stand beside him on such an important day, especially when he had all of his brothers already there, was special. As he passed O'Malley's Market, he caught his reflection in the mirror and inwardly cringed. If he was to stand for Claron, he needed to look better than he currently did. He rubbed a hand over his scraggily beard and then ran his fingers beneath his waist band, adjusting his pants around his burly middle. He never thought of himself as overweight, but perhaps it wouldn't hurt him to lose a few pounds before the big day. After all, if he was to escort the gorgeous Chloe O'Rifcan down the aisle, he wished to look his best in comparison. Not that anyone could compare to Chloe. She was one of a kind. Still, he'd attempt an effort in trimming up for the big day and see how it went.

∞

"'Twas sweet of you to ask Conor to be one of your bests." Chloe smiled at her older brother.

"'Twas a no-brainer," Claron replied. "Do you think us crazy to try and marry in two months' time?"

She grinned. "Not a'tall. I think Rhea would marry you right now if she could have everything planned already."

Claron beamed. "I still can't believe she's going to be me wife. I don't know how I ever found favor enough for that."

"Don't be so hard on yourself." Chloe shoved his shoulder. "You aren't that bad."

He laughed. "Thanks for that, sister."

"Besides, I can't wait for you two to marry so I will have more nieces and nephews to spoil. Can you imagine a babe?"

"No. Though Riley keeps filling me head about it."

"Riley?"

"With his drafts for the cottage. Always making sure we have room for Roland and the 'many wee babes' Rhea and I will be having. Seems everyone just wants the babes these days."

Chloe smiled. "Just wishing you even more happiness, brother."

"Is that even possible?" Claron shook his head in bewilderment. "If I could wish anything on anyone, it would be the way I feel when I'm with Rhea."

Chloe's heart sighed at such a sweet thought and she wondered if she'd ever find a man who felt the same way towards her. "No two people better suited than you and your Rhea." She stood. "I need to head back to me shop. I have an arrangement I need to finish. See you around, brother."

"Aye, have a care."

Chloe shoved her hands into her pockets as she followed the footpath back to her store. Conor emerged from the door as she appeared and held up a small tube of what could only be something her sister supplied him with for his hands. "Good!" she called after him and saw his shoulders shake as he chuckled and headed towards his mam's restaurant, to no doubt, check on his mother. She smiled to herself as she stepped inside her shop. Layla plopped into the stool across from her as she began sorting through her plans for the next arrangement. "Delaney hasn't texted me all day," she whined.

"He's working," Chloe pointed out.

"Aye, but he could return a text. I've seen him do it a dozen times."

"Aren't you having dinner with him tonight?"

"Aye. But that is this evening. I want a text now." Layla pouted and Chloe sighed in false aggravation.

"Am I to be surrounded by saps all day now? First Rhea, then Clary, now you. 'Tis an epidemic."

"Must be something in the stars." Layla heaved an exaggerated sigh as she motioned across the street. "Treated Conor's hands, per your request. Dreadful, they looked."

"Aye. 'Tis why I sent him to you."

"Did he tell you he's working on my stools again?"

"Aye. He did."

"I'm grateful. I was hoping to have a bit more detail in them."

"More detail?" Chloe gaped at her sister. "He carved them especially for you. You should be happy he gave them as much time and effort as he did, considering the load he's carryin'."

"He offered." Layla flipped her hair over her shoulder in annoyance as she tapped her finger nails on Chloe's counter. "I think I will go help Mammy for a bit at the café. Things have been slow this morning. Can you cover me shop while I'm out?"

"Aye."

Layla walked over to grab her purse from underneath her work counter. "I hear Murphy's throwing a bit of a party at the pub tonight. You may want to stop by and show support."

"And will you be?"

"Depends on what Delaney has planned for us." She grinned mischievously.

Chloe just shook her head as she bit back a smile. "Alright, I'll make an appearance for both our sakes."

"Thanks," Layla called over her shoulder as she made her way up the street.

Chloe sat on her stool as she submerged a piece of floral foam in a bucket of water. The spongy consistency would not only hydrate the flowers but would also help hold the arrangements shape. She snipped the edges of the flowers, placing them in a glass pitcher of water to keep hydrated while she prepped.

She set Rhea's list of flower requests inside her schedule book. She'd look over that later and see what she could order and what she'd have to substitute. If her schedule went to plan today, she'd wrap up this arrangement, the buyer would pick it up at four, she'd give Layla her rose at five, then she would head over to McCarthy's Restaurant and help Conor's mammy with the evening supper rush, and then head to Murphy's for his special pub night. She felt tired just thinking of another long evening, but when it came to her siblings, and to Conor's family, she'd do whatever she needed to help or encourage.

«CHAPTER TWO»

The balm helped, he'd admit, but now that his hands were softened, his judgment was skewed. He smoothed his palm over the tabletop once more and sighed. He'd have to come back to it. His hand was too conditioned to feel any texture differences. His calluses usually determined the texture of the wood for him, as odd as it sounded. He heard a tap on the glass door and looked up to find Riley O'Rifcan standing on the other side, shielding his hand over his eyes to peer through the glass to check whether or not Conor was inside. When he spotted him, he opened the door and walked in.

"Day to you, Conor."

"Seems I have a full day of O'Rifcans on me hands. How's she cuttin', Riley?"

Riley's eyes sparkled in pleasure as he gazed at the tabletop. He ran his hand down the grain and let out a low whistle. "Smooth as a wee baby's bottom."

"Think so? I wasn't quite sure yet."

"Aye. Nice and smooth."

Conor respected Riley's opinion. The man was a genius when it came to building. Whether it be a skyscraper or a chair, the brother knew his stuff. Confirming he was finished with the tabletop, Conor shifted it to a rack on the back wall, Riley grabbing the opposite end without having to be asked. When the wood was resting, Conor swiped his hands on his pant legs.

"I have an invite for you." Riley reached into his shirt pocket and withdrew a small envelope, embossed with metallic font and swirls. Conor's name was elegantly written and not like any invitation he'd ever received before. His brows rose as he accepted it.

"And what's this?" He flicked the tab and pulled out the small slip of stationary. "Say, now." Conor looked at Riley in surprise. "Already finished in Galway?"

"Aye." Riley beamed. "Ahead of schedule. We will be hosting a 'soft opening' for the art museum before their grand one. Basically, we have run of the place until we tell them we are finished. There will be no art yet, just a finished space full of posh and free pints."

"How could I say no to that?" Conor chuckled.

"Ah, but you would be needing a suit. 'Tis a black-tie affair."

Conor frowned. "That be the second suit I'm going to need for you O'Rifcan brothers. The lot of ye are starting to be expensive."

Riley laughed. "I take it Clary asked you to stand with him?"

"He did."

"He said he aimed to. I'm glad he did. Seems we will both be needing to find a suit for the big day."

"Would it be wrong of me to wear the same one for both occasions?" Conor asked, genuinely curious as to whether or not he could.

Riley shook his head and slapped a friendly hand on Conor's shoulder. "That be a no, I'm afraid. I guarantee our Rhea has a specific suit in mind for us."

"I was afraid you would say that. Well, I'll see what the mammy has of me da's. I know she's held onto some of his things over the years."

Riley's face sobered as Conor mentioned his father. A great man gone too soon. "I imagine she'll have something that suits you." He smiled encouragingly. "I best be on me way. You stopping by Murphy's tonight?"

"Aye. Planned on it. For a bit."

"Good. I'll see you there. Have a care."

Conor rubbed a hand over his beard and sighed. Two friends. Two suits. Two special occasions. He'd have to ask Chloe what she knows in regards to Rhea's suit choices. Though Conor wasn't hurting financially, he liked to squirrel away what he could so that he could eventually build a house on his family's land. He'd grown up on a small clearing just down from Clary's spot at Angel's Gap. But with the death of his father, a thirteen-year-old Conor and his mam had moved to town and lived in the small apartment off the restaurant. The land was still there. The house was there... empty. Even as an adult, Conor had yet to make the move. He wanted to, but the house needed work. It wasn't until the last couple of years he'd been scraping and saving every bit of money he could to put towards a fund for the place. Only Clary knew of his plans. *A dream, really*, he corrected himself. The land and house were his *dream*. His *plans* consisted of working hard and as much as possible to save up enough to make his dream a reality. Until then, he lived frugally. Two expensive suit rentals, or purchases, weren't in his budget. But for the O'Rifcan brothers, he knew he'd figure something out.

∞

Chloe threaded her fingers through her red ringlets and let them fall about her shoulders. She wasn't much for fluffing, but as the aroma of fried fish and chips emanated from her curls, she decided a shower was necessary. She'd make it quick and let her hair air dry on the way to the pub.

A few minutes later, as she rubbed a palm over the foggy mirror, her hopes of wearing a natural face for the night faded as she spotted the dark circles that tinted beneath her eyes. Sighing, she reached for her creams. Her mother would be tsking her tongue about now if she saw the current state of Chloe's face. Her mam already scolded Chloe for working too much. And though she knew Chloe was helping at McCarthy's, Sidna did not know how often. She would not be upset that Chloe helped out, but that she was tiring herself out in the process. And it was true. She was tired. She hadn't started feeling so ragged but the last few days and whatever it was, she just couldn't shake it. She offered a forced smile at the face in the mirror before turning to her wardrobe. She'd make the rounds at Murphy's Pub and then come right back home. To bed. To her cozy, comfortable, and fluffy bed. She eyed it longingly as she slipped into a little dark green dress. She was also wearing flats tonight. No heels for her sore feet.

Her phone rang, and she rushed over to her coffee table to grab it. Swiping, she answered. "Why hello there, Rhea darling. What's the craic?"

A soft giggle fluttered over the phone. "Always makes me laugh when one of you says 'craic.'"

"I know." Chloe grinned.

"Well, I am headed back to Castlebrook from work. Delaney closed up shop a bit early today. Said something about an evening with Layla."

"Did he now? Closing early is not our Mr. Hawkins' usual style."

"No. It's not," Rhea agreed. "It's been quite fun to see him transforming into... well, a normal person. Don't tell him I said that. It would probably hurt his feelings."

"Your secret is safe with me. Besides, we all see how much he's changed since pairing with Layla. As has she. Some."

"Some." Rhea chuckled. "Anyways, I wanted to see if you were attending Murphy's big celebration tonight?"

"Getting myself dressed as we speak."

"Oh good. Claron had mentioned we should go. I just wanted to see who all would be there. I'd still go, regardless," she amended, not wanting to think Claron was forcing her to attend. "I'd just rather hang with you and Heidi tonight than a rowdy bar full of people."

"I understand, love. I'm feeling much like that myself. A bit tired today."

"That's because you work too hard."

"Says the woman who is just now leaving the office two hours past the time her boss dismissed her."

"Good point."

Chloe could hear the sounds of driving in the background as Rhea made her way towards Sidna's Bed and Breakfast. Her designated suite still remained her substitute housing when she stayed in Castlebrook. Though Chloe knew Layla harped on Clary and Rhea for the superfluous situation, it suited the two love birds just fine. They wished to keep their love for one another pure until their marriage, and no one could fault them for such a romantic gesture. Besides that,

Chloe's parents had grown rather fond of having Rhea staying with them on the weekends. She'd quickly become like a daughter to them, and Chloe knew her mother enjoyed the extra company Rhea provided. Chloe's Da had Roland, Rhea's grandfather, as regular company, so it was only fitting her mam had someone to chat with too. Chloe tuned back into Rhea's conversation.

"So you think you can pencil that in?"

"I'm sorry, what? I trailed in thought a moment."

"Dress fittings, next week. My mom flies in on Tuesday, and she wants to hit the ground running. Layla's already made appointments at several bridal shops in Limerick for us to stop at on Friday. Aunt Grace is even coming down from Galway to join us."

"Friday is fine. I will make a note of it. Exciting it is, thinking of a pretty dress for your big day."

"You're going to look so beautiful."

"Shouldn't I be telling you that?" Chloe asked on a laugh.

"And yet another good point. Beauty and brains. My goodness, Chloe O'Rifcan, how are you still single?" Rhea teased.

"'Tis the workaholic part that turns them off," Chloe admitted with a bit of sarcasm.

Rhea laughed. "You know, I could help with that. I'm an excellent matchmaker. As is evident by Layla and Delaney."

"You did not set that up. Fate did. And you best be careful taking credit for her work, Rhea Conners," Chloe playfully warned.

"Oh, she likes my help," Rhea added. "Maybe."

Laughing, Chloe walked towards the small kitchenette in her efficiency and poured a glass of water. "You headed straight to Clary's?"

"No. I was going to come pick you up."

Surprised, but pleased at the offer, Chloe grinned. "Who needs a man when I have you, Rhea love?"

"I'm an enabler."

Snorting before she laughed, Chloe covered her mouth to compose herself. "Hurry up ye floozie and let's go out on the lash." She hung up and stuffed her phone in her purse. Thankful to end her long day with a good friend, Chloe checked her look once more before heading out the door to wait for Rhea.

∞

"'Tis about time you showed up, lad. I was beginning to feel offended." Murphy O'Rifcan slid a pint in front of Conor and extended his hand for a quick shake. "The day been hard on ya?"

"Just long. Glad to be celebratin' you tonight."

"Aye. As you should be. As should everyone here." Murphy winked at a pretty brunette as he slid her a freshly made drink across the bar top. A slap sounded on his shoulder as Piper walked up and then slid a towel over the damp bar.

"Conor," she greeted warmly.

"I see he's recruited you for his big night, Piper dear." Conor toasted towards her as he took his first sip.

"Muprhy's always beggin' for me help these days. Seems he can't quite operate without me." She rested her elbow on Murphy's shoulder as the brother rolled his eyes.

"My pub has been here for ten years, love. How long have you worked here?"

"I don't," she reminded him smugly. "Just when you beg me to help."

Murphy, tongue in cheek, kept his last remark to himself as Piper grinned and walked off with more sass than she'd previously possessed. "She trouble for you?" Conor asked.

"No," Murphy replied on a sigh. "And yes."

Conor chuckled.

"Still attempting to recruit her from Galway, but she's diggin' her feet in over there the more I ask. We will see. The pub she operates in Galway is serving Riley's fancy gatherin'. We'll see how she feels after that."

"You helping her?"

Murphy shook his head. "I'm a guest." His face broke into a wide smile. "I will be dressed in me finest, boyo." He held a hand to his chest proudly.

"Not a lass in Galway will be safe from those charms." Conor laughed, pounding his fist on the bar as Murphy joined in.

"Creating a ruckus, are we?" Claron slid onto the stool next to Conor and nodded in greeting. "I'll have a plain, brother." Without hesitation, Murphy began preparing Claron a drink.

"You alone? Our Rhea grew smart finally, did she?" Murphy teased, sliding the freshly kegged pint Claron's direction.

"She's on her way. Stopped to pick up Chloe."

"Ah. A sweetheart, your Rhea."

Claron took a sip of his beer and nodded. "Aye. She is."

"She is what?" Rhea's voice interrupted as she leaned down and kissed Claron's cheek in welcome and gently patted Conor's back. "How are you gentlemen this evening?"

Conor looked up and smiled, his gaze carrying towards Chloe as she hopped onto the stool on the other side of him. "Hi there, gingernut."

Her smile was faint, but friendly as she rested her elbows on the bar. "Conor. Glad to see you make it out tonight."

"Same to you. That be a pretty dress ye're wearin'."

"Thanks." Chloe tapped her knuckles on the bar and Murphy slid a glass in front of her. "I am forever grateful, brother." She took a long and satisfying sip.

"You look completely knackered, little sister." Murphy's brows furrowed in concern as Chloe shrugged her shoulders. "No, really." He snapped at Claron and both brothers eyed their sister closely. Chloe held up her hand to ward off their attention.

"I be fine. Just a long day."

"Been workin' herself to the bone, she has," Conor added and winced at the slap on his arm.

"Says the fool of a man sitting next to me, busted knuckles and all."

"You do look tired," Rhea admitted.

"No woman, no matter how exhausted, likes to hear she looks it," Chloe told them.

"That's true," Rhea conceded. "You still look lovely, Chloe. You're just not your usual spunky self."

The sister flushed.

"Nothing to get scundered about." Conor assured her with a pat to the hand. "Just concerned for our favorite coppertop."

"Well, please do not worry over me. Tonight is our Murphy's night to shine, right brother?"

Murphy beamed. "That it is. Best you all remember it." He poured himself his own pint and slid under the bar door and popped up next to Rhea. "Piper on the kegs!" He called towards the petite blonde as she worked her way down the bar. "I am officially handing over the reigns for the night. Now, Rhea love, let me take you for a spin."

Claron did not object and instead took Rhea's glass from her hand and set it on the bar.

"'Tis a lively tune." Conor's foot had already started tapping and he looked to Chloe with a grin. "Best not to waste it." He grabbed her hand and pulled her from her stupor until he had her laughing and twirling alongside Murphy and Rhea.

«CHAPTER THREE»

"Late night, love?" her mother's voice cut through the haze in her mind like a lighthouse in the fog. Chloe cupped her coffee in her hands and inhaled deeply as her the familiar sounds of her mother floating about the kitchen and prepping for her day's work soothed her.

"A bit. I did not intend to stay at the pub as long as I did, but Murphy was looking to be spoiled, so we all acquiesced. I rode with Rhea, and we stopped by here before she was to take me home so I could borrow a top of hers, and I was just so knackered, I stayed."

Sidna ran a soothing hand over Chloe's red curls. "Always welcome. 'Tis your home, after all."

"Thank, Mam."

"Something else bothering you?" Sidna prodded, removing several pots and pans from a cupboard beneath the work island.

"No."

"Chloe Múireann, don't think you can fool your mammy now," Sidna warned. "I see something wrong with ye. Best tell me."

"You'll only fret. And there be no reason to."

"I'll be the judge of that. Now, tell me."

Chloe gently set her coffee mug on the island counter and threaded her hands together. "I'm not feeling my full self... As if I'm on the brink of being sickly." She held up her hand to prevent her mother from interrupting. "I've been taking me vitamins. I just can't seem to shake this... tiredness. My body feels sluggish. And I can't be this way right now. Not with planning for Rhea and Clary's wedding or helping Mrs. McCarthy."

Sidna frowned as she listened. "Perhaps it is your body's way of telling you to rest. Have you ever thought of that? I've seen you lately, runnin' here and there and everywhere. A body needs rest, Chloe dear, and yours is screamin' at you to do so. Best listen to it. What's on your plate for today?"

"Planning to help at McCarthy's this morning for a bit. I don't have any scheduled arrangements, so it will just be working in the store today. Then I plan to help with the evening rush over at McCarthy's."

"I'll send Emily to help Mammy McCarthy both this morning and this evening. Layla can man the store, and you can take a rest."

"Mam—"

"Don't Mammy me, love. A mam knows when her child needs care. You will take it when it's offered. Now off you go. Go home. Take a long bath and relax."

Knowing it was a losing battle to argue with her mother, Chloe slid to her feet. "Alright. As you wish."

Sidna's lips tilted into a loving smile. "If I so much as catch a glimpse of that redhead before supper, you'll be answering to yer Da. Hear me?"

"Aye, Mam." Chloe kissed her on the cheek as she headed out the door. Rhea had long since left the B&B to head back to Limerick for work and since Chloe did not have to rush to ready herself for the morning, she did as her mother suggested, nay *demanded*, she do. She made the short walk up the footpath towards the little blue shop on the corner owned by the wonderful Mrs. O'Donoghue. The two-story building had seen better years, but the framework was strong enough to not only serve as Mrs. O'Donoghue's dress shop, but also Chloe's apartment above it. Years ago, when the building operated as a shoe store, the old cobbler, Mr. Ennison, had lived above his work, converting the entire upper story into a small apartment. The place had not been used in decades until Mrs. O'Donoghue agreed to let Chloe rent it out. Though Chloe did not pay rent. Instead, the agreement was that she'd fix it up and take care of it, and that 'twas good enough for Mrs. O'Donoghue. And she'd done just that.

As she walked up the short flight of stairs that wrapped around the rear of the building, Chloe opened her door to the sweet and comforting smell of home. She loved the brightness of the place. And though it was now a home, it still held the floor to ceiling storefront windows that overlooked Castlebrook's main drag. She'd had to make custom curtains for the wall, and Conor had made her a sturdy rod to hold them. But on days of sunshine or even of heavy rains, it was nice to let the outdoors in. The wooden floors, which she had sanded down to a smooth and polished finish with Conor's help, creaked under her feet as she headed towards the small bathroom that housed a luxurious claw foot tub, courtesy of her brother Riley's artistic touch. She turned the water on, letting the steam rise about the room as she deliberated over which of Layla's concoctions she wished to toss in. To have such a luxury as a long morning bath, Chloe felt she needed to enjoy it as much as possible. But she wasn't quite sure what to do. Should she read? Listen to music? Have a glass of wine? It was morning, she chided herself, she couldn't indulge at this time. Champagne would have been a better substitute, but she didn't have any on hand. As her feet hit the hot water, she realized she needed absolutely nothing else. The water eased her tired muscles, exfoliated her skin, and opened her airway as she dropped some of Layla's bath salts into the water. She watched them slowly dissolve and their magic of conditioning and softening her skin began. She'd soak for a half hour, she told herself, and then she'd set about working on one of her own little projects around the house. An hour and a half later, she awoke to the sound of horn blasting on the street and a tub of cold water.

∞

Conor penciled down the last measurement and slipped the chiseled wooden utensil behind his ear. He hooked his tape measure onto his belt loop and stepped outside the small cottage at Angel's Gap and paused to soak in the view. Claron had one of the best spots in County Clare sitting on the cliffs of Angel's Gap. The small cottage, having belonged to Claron's grandparents, was passed to Claron years ago, when they were still boys. Conor smirked at the memory of Claron's first night living in the house by himself. He, Riley, and Conor thought it'd be grand to have a stag night. At seventeen, eighteen, and nineteen years old, the night consisted of mainly drinking and telling old tales. Not much had changed when the three of them still got together. He supposed they'd be planning a different kind of stag night for Clary now that he and Rhea were about to wed. Conor made a mental note to discuss the matter with Riley.

As he stepped off the porch stoop, he spotted Chloe's red hair amongst the emerald grass under the tree near the cliff's edge. Curious, Conor walked towards her.

"Convening with the fairies, are we?" he asked, seeing her shoulders slightly jump in surprise before she turned.

She greeted him with her usual sweet smile. "I find they are experts when it comes to flowers. I'd be a fool to ignore them."

"Aye. I suppose you would. But don't you know that the real fairy mound be over in that direction?" He pointed to the pastureland down the hill.

"Your land?" she asked, amused. "And how do you know that's where the fairy prince lives?"

"Well, I've seen him," Conor admitted with a wink. "Likes to come out at the full moon and gawk over pretty redheads."

Chloe grinned as her gaze moved back towards the cliffs, the light breeze ruffling her hair.

Conor eased onto the ground beside her and leaned back on his hands, his legs splayed in front of him. "You not up at the store today?"

"No. I've been banished. By me Mam."

"Whatever for?"

Chloe flushed a bit. "I was a wee bit tired this morning and she took to that like a madwoman, reorganizing my day. So here I sit, borrowing Clary's cliffs. Nothing to do but listen to the River Shannon, soak up sunshine, and feel the breeze. I've had worse days."

"Aye. Not a bad schedule, I'd say." Chloe eyed the pencil behind his ear.

"And what are you doing here at Angel's Gap?"

"Oh, measuring a space for Clary. Seems the area around the fireplace won't be changin' much, but he wished to add some bookcases on either side."

"Another project." Chloe's brow quirked. "Your days of working at the restaurant might be over if you keep up this work load."

"Me Mam and I discussed the matter. I'd be the eejit if I let such work pass me by. She agrees and has been looking for more help."

"Do you miss it?" Chloe asked.

"A bit. Though I've always enjoyed working with me hands, whether cooking or building. Besides, I make more building."

"And that's important to you now?" Chloe asked, a hint of distaste in her voice at the thought of Conor becoming greedy. It wasn't in his nature.

"A bit. Still saving for my dream."

"And what dream is that?"

He blushed under the extra scrutiny, his ruddy face turning towards his family's land. "So I can set that place to rights."

"You wish to buy it? I thought you already owned it?"

"Own? Aye. In a way. Me Mammy owns it still, but the house has been vacant since we moved to the restaurant."

"Why didn't she rent it out? Or sell it? I know that would have been helpful for you two at some point during the years."

"Aye, no doubt. But it's land. Family land. Belonged to me Mam's da. She wouldn't dream of selling it. Yet, she never wanted to stay at that house since me Da left. Too many memories, I suppose."

Chloe nodded in understanding. "And you want to fix up the house?"

"No. I want to tear it down," Conor clarified, grinning at her surprised face. "And build something new."

A slow smile spread over her lips as she sighed. "I believe you can do just that, Conor."

"'Tis but a dream. I have a ways to go yet."

"Don't you know these cliffs are where dreams come true?" Chloe grinned as they heard some sort of farm equipment come to life and knew Claron was tending to his fields.

Conor's eyes set upon the steep cliff in front of them, the grass softly whispering as the wind blew through its blades. "I remember sitting here with Clary through the years. Mostly when we were young and I could walk over. Your grands," he smiled. "They'd set us to work, digging potatoes, milking cows, hauling buckets of feed. Whatever task they needed to find to occupy us young lads. Your nanny was the kindest lass. I loved coming over just to have her fuss over me." His smile softened, and then, as if embarrassed, he cleared his throat and leaned forward. "I better get to it." He hefted himself to his feet as Chloe handed him the tape measure that'd slipped from his belt.

"I think it a grand dream, Conor. Don't give up on it, hm?"

"What be your dream, Chloe?" He crossed his arms and waited patiently for her to answer. Her green eyes darted out towards the cliffs again.

"To continue working with flowers, settle down, and have a family."

"A good dream," Conor told her. "How 'bout we shake on it?"

"What?" She looked up at him confused.

"I won't give up on my dream if you don't give up on yours?" He held his hand down to her. He waved it at her and waited until she clasped it.

"My dream has a ways to go yet as well. But deal," she said, giving his hand a firm shake. Her lips split into a nervous smile. "Don't think I've ever told anyone that dream before."

"I haven't either," Conor admitted. "I imagine the cliffs will keep our secrets and dreams to themselves. They've done so for centuries for others."

Chloe gave him a grateful look that had him wondering why she'd think it so odd for her to wish for a family of her own. What had made Chloe O'Rifcan feel like it was more of a dream than a reality for her?

"Best continue your day of dabbling, coppertop, or Mammy Sidna will be on your scent." He heard her laugh as he headed back towards the cottage and to his lorry. When he opened the door and slid one leg inside, he paused a moment to glance back towards the cliffs. He lifted his phone and snapped a picture of Chloe sitting there. A sight. A beautiful touch of red amongst the green, all so at ease under the tree. Chloe looked much like the petals she tended: graceful and beautiful. But, he noted, also a bit delicate. And delicate was not a word typically used to describe Chloe O'Rifcan. Yet, he found he liked that it did now.

∞

It was noon, and she'd run out of things to do. As far as a day of rest goes, she'd enjoyed it. But it was only noon. She still had half the day, and she was completely clueless as to what to do with herself. She felt the day wasting away. She could organize her shop, but Layla would hover and accuse of her working. She could visit Clary next milking, but again, he'd shoo her away because she would want to help. Murphy. She snapped her fingers as if she had a brilliant idea and walked towards the pub. Of all her siblings, she knew Murphy would either give her ideas on how to spend her day or allow her to mingle at the pub and feel useful without overdoing it.

She walked inside to the sounds of shouting coming from the storeroom and walked to the door standing ajar.

"Stubbornness has nothing to do with it, Murphy O'Rifcan!" An exasperated Piper stormed towards the door and spotted Chloe. She did not hide her annoyed expression, but instead pointed a finger at Chloe, as if being an O'Rifcan at that very moment deserved her wrath. "I am cut to the onions with your brother!" Piper exited in a huff and Chloe could hear the cute blonde stacking the freshly washed glasses behind the bar with more force than was necessary.

Murphy emerged from the cooler, his hands carrying two crates of beer. His brows rose at seeing Chloe. "Sister."

"What, pray tell, have you done to poor Piper?" Chloe asked.

A sly smile spread over Murphy's face. "She only be angry because she knows I'm right."

"Eejit!" Piper's voice carried from the other room and had him laughing.

"Still trying to recruit her?" Chloe asked.

"Aye. After her running things last night, I think she saw how much MY PUB," he began to yell, "is better than the one she runs in Galway."

"We'll bloody see about that come Riley's opening." Piper walked towards them and took the top crate off Murphy's load.

"A posh event like Riley's is nothing compared to the locals here in Castlebrook. They won't hold a candle."

"We'll have to see about that, now won't we?"

"I will see, because I will be there. As a guest, of course." Murphy winked at Piper and only made her steam more as she continued her work. He then turned his attention towards Chloe.

"So, what's the story with you, sister? Why you here?"

"I'm bored out of me mind," Chloe admitted. "Mam accused me of working too hard, so she handed off all me responsibilities. I've taken a long bath. A long walk to Clary's and back. And now I've run out of things to do. I was hoping you could put me to work and keep shut about it."

Murphy laughed. "Always work around here, but to cross Mammy could be the death of me."

Chloe frowned. "Murphy, there has to be something. I'll even have a pint while doing it so it seems as if I'm just visiting and keeping me hands busy."

Piper walked up and handed Chloe a basket of freshly washed bar towels. "Fold."

Chloe nodded appreciatively as she sat on a stool and began to neatly fold the towels. "How many towels do you use a night, Murphy? My goodness, there must be a hundred here."

"About half that. That be a couple days' worth," he replied.

"'Tis lunch time, you could head to Mammy's for a bite or to McCarthy's."

"Not hungry." Chloe stacked a fresh towel on her previous one.

"Leave her be, Murphy. Do you always have to pester?" Piper jibed.

"Yes," Chloe and Murphy replied at the same time and smiled at one another.

"When do you head back to Galway, Piper?" Chloe asked.

"Two."

"She wouldn't have to if she worked here," Murphy pointed out.

Piper rolled her eyes as she ignored him and walked over to take half of the towels Chloe had finished and stocked them beneath the bar.

"I'm slowly winning her over," Murphy added in a stage whisper.

"Looks like it," Chloe replied, her sarcasm making Piper snicker. She finished the last of the towels and sighed. "Well, that was a nice filler."

"Could always try Clary. He's always got work piling up."

"I thought about that, but he'd only treat me like a delicate flower or refuse to let me exert myself."

"True."

"Layla is under orders to not let me in the shop."

Murphy grimaced. "And crossing Layla would be like crossing the River Shannon in a storm."

"Aye. Agreed." Chloe rested her chin in her hands.

"What of Conor? He's been busy as of late. Go bother him." Murphy grinned. "Not that you're bothering me..."

"Right." Chloe smirked at his honesty, knowing her brother did cherish the quiet times he had at the pub each afternoon before the evening rush.

"Already talked with Conor. He was at Clary's earlier, taking his measurements."

"Ah, see, he's probably back at his shop."

"'Tis not fair for me to bother him twice today."

"Is it so hard to watch the telly for an afternoon? Or sleep? Or—" Murphy paused for dramatic effect. "This would be the opportune time for you to have a lad to go do things with. Have him take you to the city for some fun."

"Aye, well we know that isn't happening, so my choices are limited for today. And I don't want to sleep the day away or watch the telly."

"Then I don't know what to tell you, sister." He heaved an exasperated sigh and looked to Piper pleadingly.

Piper reached under the bar and grabbed her purse. "Come along, Chloe. I could eat the twelve apostles. Let's leave this annoying prawn and go fetch a bite, hm?"

"You're only doing this because you feel sorry for me," Chloe pointed out.

KATHARINE E. HAMILTON

"Not so. I'm tired of Murphy. You'd be doing *me* a favor." Piper winked at her as Chloe slid off the stool to her feet.

"He is a bit cheeky today, isn't he?" Chloe agreed.

"Aye. He always is." Piper opened the door to the sunshine and Chloe's mood instantly brightened when they walked towards her mam's café.

"I appreciate you taking a break," Chloe said.

"I needed some fresh air," Piper told her. "He's been houndin' me all mornin'."

"Is he gaining ground?" Chloe asked.

"A bit. Part of me knows it would be a lovely change to come to Castlebrook, but I have a good reputation in Galway. I make a decent living there. It would be hard to give up. Plus, there are perks to living in the city."

"I've never wished to leave Castlebrook on a permanent basis, but I'm wondering if I'm reaching the point that I need to for a bit."

Surprised, Piper turned to the youngest O'Rifcan. "Why's that?"

"You'll think me a stook."

"I doubt that," Piper replied. "Tell me."

"All my siblings falling in love and finding their persons... makes me wonder if I ever will here in Castlebrook or should I go somewhere else for a bit. Be adventurous. Find a fella somewhere and then settle here."

"But who's to say he would want to settle in Castlebrook?"

"There is that. And who's to say I'd even find a fella."

"I don't imagine that part would be hard." Piper grinned at her. "Plenty of men who'd turn a glad eye at a beauty like you."

Chloe flushed. "Thanks, though I'm not so sure. Besides, my plate is full here. Not with men," she quickly added, seeing the line of thinking on Piper's face. "With work and family. Rhea's wedding plans. Riley's big opening. I don't see a possibility that I could sneak away any time soon."

"You could always come up to Galway for the weekend, stay with me. We could go out. I could introduce you to some of me friends." Piper found them a table in the courtyard and Lorena walked over and placed menus in front of them with a gentle pat to Chloe's shoulder.

"I'll think on it. Thanks." Chloe leaned back in her chair and soaked up the sun as it filtered through the clouds. She smelled her mam's bread and her stomach grumbled.

"I hear ya." Piper chuckled. "Your mam's bread is phenomenal. I believe I've gained weight since I began coming here so frequently."

"Don't tell her that. 'Twill only encourage her to feed you even more." Chloe grinned as their dishes were placed in front of them and both women dug in heartily.

«CHAPTER FOUR»

Conor made the note on the pad he kept in his shirt pocket. "Not sure when I can make that trip, but I'll try to squeeze it in."

Layla beamed and clasped her hands together on top of her work counter. "I knew you would. My stools will be the prettiest in County Clare."

Somewhat disappointed she didn't think they already were, Conor loaded them on his broad shoulders and walked towards the door. Layla held the door open as he edged outside.

"Conor? What on Earth you doing?" Chloe and Piper walked towards him as he set the stools in the back of his lorry.

Layla darted over to the truck and peeked over the edge, drawing her sister's attention to her stools. "Aren't they lovely, Chloe?"

"They are."

Piper let out a low whistle as she ran a hand over the intricately carved legs. "I've never seen work like this. Absolutely stunning."

Conor flushed under the extra attention and Chloe smiled proudly at him, her brow furrowing slightly at the look of disappointment that crossed over his face. "Why are you taking them back?"

"Oh," Layla swung her hair over her shoulder before she spoke. "I asked Conor to tile the seats. Won't that look pretty? The pretty tile work from Adare."

"Adare?" Chloe asked. "But that's a bit of a drive just for tile people plan to put their rear ends on."

Layla scowled. "It's what I want," Layla stated. "And so Conor said he'd do it."

"They're already beautiful." Chloe insisted.

"But I want the tile," Layla added. "And so, I'm willing to wait for them to be extra beautiful." She playfully kissed Conor's cheek before darting back into the store.

"Conor—" Chloe began to protest but halted at his raised hand.

"I already told her I don't mind."

"But—"

"I want her to love them," Conor said. "If tile from Adare does that, then tile from Adare it shall be."

"You may talk to Riley," Chloe told him. "I know he bought some for Clary's house. He might have extra. It would save you the trip."

"I actually already made that call," Conor told her. "And he doesn't as of right now. But that's okay."

"I'd take these off your hands right now for double what she's paying you, Piper pitched in, her face serious.

Conor chuckled and then sobered when he caught her expression. "Oh, well, I couldn't do that to Layla. I could make you some though. Might be a while, but I could add it to the list."

"I'll get back to you," Piper told him. "But I definitely wouldn't mind a set of these in my flat."

Chloe smiled at the idea and gently rested a hand on Conor's arm. Her touch surprised him, and he looked down at her kind face. "You're a saint, Conor McCarthy. There's no doubting it."

"And my offer still stands. If she decides she doesn't want them, I do. Tile or no tile," Piper said.

"On with ye." He waved them away. "A man would float away with the two of you around for long. I can already feel me head swellin'."

Piper patted him on the shoulder as she and Chloe continued on their way towards Murphy's Pub. "Have a pint for me!" Conor called after them. He reached into the bed of his lorry and grabbed some rope and began tying down Layla's stools. If he left now, he could possibly fit a trip to Adare in for the day and be back in plenty of time to finish working on the chairs he'd started for Clary's table.

"Conor." A breathless Chloe appeared at his side.

"Something wrong, coppertop?" Concerned, he waited until she caught her breath.

She shook her head. "No, I just ran from the pub is all. I wanted to see if you needed any help today?"

"Help?" His brows furrowed.

"Aye. Does no one wish for service these days?" She fisted her hands on her hips.

He smirked. "Aren't you supposed to be resting?"

"Aye. I am. But I'm feeling much better and want to be of use. Somewhere."

"Ah." Conor scratched his beard. "Well, I was debating on a trip to Adare."

"I'll go with you." She all but jumped at the chance and he laughed.

"Alright, have it your way then. I aim for it to be a quick trip."

"'Tis fine." She smiled as she hopped into his passenger seat and buckled up faster than he could open his door. Chuckling, he buckled his safety belt.

"'Twill be nice to have some company. I'm not used to having a pretty lass riding shotgun, as Rhea says."

Chloe grinned. "I thank ye for letting me. I haven't been to Adare in quite some time. 'Twill be nice to see it."

"Aye. Well then, off we go now." He cranked the engine and on the second try it sputtered to life. He reached over towards the dashboard in front of Chloe and removed the stacks of invoices and receipts he'd piled up there. His lorry wasn't exactly primed for carrying a passenger, much less a lass. Embarrassed, he caught sight of an empty cup on the floorboard next to her feet. He leaned to reach for it and she swatted his hand.

"Stop frettin', Conor. Your lorry is fine."

When he made the turn to leave Castlebrook, he relaxed and listened as Chloe began to hum while she stared out the window.

∞

Conor pulled to a stop and parked in front of a small hardware store in the Adare Heritage Centre and Chloe hopped out. "This be where you find your tiles?"

Conor nodded. "Usually. If they don't have any, I'll go to 'ol McDougal and see what he has on hand."

Conor opened the glass door and a tiny bell jingled at their entrance. Chloe walked inside and her eyes adjusted to the dimly lit room. An elderly woman, small in stature glanced up from a game of Solitaire spread on the sales counter. "Conor McCarthy come today, has he?" She smiled and stood, walking around the counter to embrace Conor. Chloe watched as his burly arms swallowed the small woman in a tight hug. He didn't release her until she patted his back. "Strong man you have there, lass." She winked at Chloe as she placed her hands on her hips. "What can I do ye for, Conor?"

"Needing some tiles. Happen to have some on hand?"

She frowned. "Ah, that'd be a no. That shiny architect O'Rifcan bought me out last. I have yet to replenish."

"Riley," Conor supplied the name and the woman nodded.

"Not that I mind him coming for tiles. Nice to look at, that one. But I'm afraid that means I can't help you. And we both know 'tis you who has me heart, love." She winked at him as she went back around the counter and perched on her stool.

Conor stroked his beard a moment as his eyes traveled around the room. They settled upon a cooling case in front of the register. He fetched two minerals and placed them on the counter, tossing some money down as well. He looked to Chloe. "Up for a little longer of a trip?"

She shrugged. "I've got the day." She smiled.

"Of course she doesn't mind," the woman added. "'Tis a lucky lass to spend the day with you, Conor. I know I'd jump at the chance if I were forty years younger."

Chloe grinned as Conor blushed. He handed Chloe one of the minerals.

"What is yer name?" Chloe extended her hand.

"Maureen. Of the O'Clare Clan. Been in Adare all me life. Don't plan to leave."

"Chloe O'Rifcan."

The woman's eyes brightened. "The shiny architect a brother now?"

"Aye, he is."

"Nice looking bunch the lot of ye."

"Sweet of you to say." Chloe looked up at Conor. "Ready?"

"Aye. When you are, lass."

"Conor McCarthy, you don't be a stranger now. Does me heart good to see you. Tell your mam a hello."

"Will do."

"I like yer lass. Bring by again." She waved them away before either of them could correct her and went back to her game. Chloe stepped back into the sunshine and took a drink of the refreshing mineral, the sweet carbonation teasing her tongue as it bubbled down her throat.

"McDougal's it is then." Conor surprised her by opening her door, but she slid in without comment. When he turned the engine a couple of times to crank, they backed out and back onto the N21 and heading to the outskirts of Adare. "On another day I'd treat you to some fish and chips, but seeing as you've already eaten, we'll just bother McDougal for a bit and be on our way. Unless you have a mouth on ye?" Conor glanced her direction and she shook her head.

"Not yet. I might be needing a snack for the ride home, but I'm fine just now."

"Alright."

"Conor," Chloe turned in her seat to face him and his brows rose in question as she studied him.

"You realize this be the first time you and I have gone somewhere together, just the two of us."

"Aye."

Chloe tucked her foot under her leg as she relaxed against the seat. "Why is that?"

"Business, I suppose."

"Aye, I guess that's part of it. We've been friends our whole lives... well, my whole life, seeing as you're older than me."

He smirked. "Not that much older."

"Several years you have on me," Chloe countered. "Clary's age, are you not? Or Riley's? I can't ever remember."

"Clary's."

"I thought so." She studied him some more and saw him fidget.

"Why are you starin' at me?" He lightly nudged her knee as she laughed.

"Not starin', just studying."

"Well, knock it off. Yer makin' me nervous."

"Why?" Grinning, she leaned her elbow on the center console and rested her chin in her hand, her eyes staring a hole into the side of his face.

He placed his roughened palm on her face and nudged her back to her chair. They both laughed.

"You planning on attending Riley's big night?"

"I am. Though I've got to find a suit for it. Not sure where to go for that."

"You should ask Delaney," Chloe suggested. "He's a man of many suits. I'm sure he'd be able to tell you."

"I have a feelin' our Mr. Delaney's budget is a bit different than mine," Conor admitted.

"True," Chloe agreed. "No telling how much his fancy suits cost. We could look today, if you like? We be near Limerick anyhow, and I can help you."

Embarrassed at the thought of trying on suits in front of Chloe, Conor shook his head. "No thanks. I'll come by one."

"Conor," Chloe tilted her head and narrowed her gaze at him. "You might as well take care of it whilst we're in the city. You know you will not have the time, nor make the time later, to do it."

She saw her argument sink in and dread covered his face as he nodded. "You're probably right about that."

"'Tis a shame one of me brothers doesn't have a suit you could borrow." She saw hurt flash in his eyes and was surprised that her comment caused such a feeling. "Something wrong?"

He shook his head as he turned down a dirt path leading to a thatched roof cottage at the end of the lane.

"Not sure if any of me brothers own a suit, minus Riley. Though Declan may have his from his wedding." Chloe continued. "I imagine they're all in the same boat you are in, searching for one and all."

She saw his shoulders relax at her words and realized he may have taken insult at her previous response. "What color suit do you think you will want?"

"I think I will shop for some tiles first and put off a suit as long as possible."

"Conor—" She chided.

He turned and faced her. "Stop naggin' me, woman. One task at a time. And findin' a suit is not me top priority at the moment."

"Aye, that is true. Spoilin' Layla more than she already is seems to be the current task."

"'Tis just tile," Conor replied.

"'Tis just ridiculous."

He tapped her chin up with his finger and stared her in the eyes. "Best not be hard on Layla, she only be wanting her shop to look pretty. She has her tastes. I'm glad to help her shape her store into what she wants it to be."

Chloe opened her mouth to reply, but he narrowed his eyes at her as he continued. "Your taste, my taste, and even Piper's taste may differ from Layla's, but that doesn't mean we can't take the time to make her stools better."

"They're already good," Chloe challenged and waved her hand towards the back of the truck.

Conor chuckled. "And it warms me heart to hear you say that. I happen to like them as is myself. But they're not for us, now are they?"

Chloe rolled her eyes and sighed. "I suppose you're right. Just seems Layla snaps and everyone, every man," she amended, "snaps to do her biddin'."

Conor's eyes flashed and Chloe saw a spark of temper settle there, the sight of it foreign on his friendly face. "Chloe O'Rifcan, if you think for one second I be doing this for Layla because she has a way with me, you best rethink. I be doing this because she's paying me to do so. Now, Clary would be a different story. His house is his dream and I'd do anything to help him and Rhea build their dream. But Layla, these are just stools. 'Tis just a job. If she be willing to pay for the time and tile, then time and tile she gets. I'd hope you'd know me better than to think me one of the lads chasing after Layla O'Rifcan."

Chloe heaved a heavy breath of remorse. "I know you're not. I'm just a wee bit aggravated with her is all, and I'm sorry. I've taken it out on you."

"I appreciate you being aggravated on me behalf, but 'tis unnecessary."

He offered his usual cheery smile and she nodded. "Now, hold onto yer locks, lass, because Mr. McDougal likes pretty coppertops."

Chloe laughed as they stepped out of the vehicle and an old man awaited them on the porch of his cottage.

∞

And Mr. McDougal did *love* Chloe. Connor grinned as the younger sister lightly kissed the man's cheek in farewell, the man's hand lingering at her waist longer than necessary. Chloe was a good sport as she slipped away and walked towards Conor. She handed him the bag of tile in her hands. "Extra," she told him. "In case some of the others break."

Conor peeked into the bag and his eyes widened. "This be three whole sets."

She wriggled her eyebrows. "He likes me."

"I'd say so." Conor chuckled as he placed the tiles in his backseat and then hopped into the truck. "I'll need to bring you every time I come see him.

"I'd like that. Has been a fun trip."

Pleased, Conor headed down Mr. McDougal's drive and back towards Limerick.

"So I'm thinking if we head towards Rhea's flat, there are a few shops in the area that we might could find you a suit."

He groaned.

"Conor," her voice scolding, "we've been through this. Best to take care of it now than later."

"You're worse than me mammy."

She punched his shoulder and he laughed. "Must be why she likes you so much."

"Or it could be because I'm charming," Chloe retorted.

"You're an O'Rifcan, charming is in yer blood."

Chloe grinned at that and pointed towards the exit that would lead them to downtown Limerick.

"Should we call upon Rhea and Heidi whilst here?"

He shook his head. "I do not wish to have an audience for trying on suits."

"Ah, but then you would have the seal of approval from three beautiful women instead of just one."

Conor snickered. "As if I need the approval of anyone. I know I'll be stunningly handsome."

She giggled. "No doubt. No doubt. But 'twould be nice to see them."

Conor sighed. "Alright, give them a ring. But don't say anything about suit buyin'. See when they're free and we will meet them somewhere."

Chloe phoned Rhea.

"Hey, Chloe," Rhea greeted, her voice on speaker phone as Chloe allowed Conor in on the conversation.

"Hi there, Rhea darling. Chloe and Conor here on our way home from Adare."

"Hi, Conor," Rhea added.

"Hello, lovely Rhea."

"We be after a suit for Conor for Riley's big museum debut."

Conor's intake of breath had Chloe smirking as he shook his head in bewilderment at going against their agreement.

"We are in Limerick and wondered if you and Heidi would fancy a meet up."

"Oh, yay!" Rhea's voice held warmth. "There's a great tailor's shop just up the block from my apartment. Dandy's I think is the name."

"Dandy's?" Conor replied quickly, appalled, and had both women laughing.

"Trust me, it's a good place, despite the name. Heidi and I will meet you there."

"Sounds perfect." Chloe hung up.

"And now I have the audience I didn't want."

"Oh it will be grand, just you wait and see," Chloe assured him. She pointed as they pulled to the front of the shop Rhea suggested, the sign boasting of the best fit in the city.

Rhea and Heidi waited out front and waved to them as they parked along the footpath. Chloe was greeted with warm hugs and then both women eyed Conor. Rhea linked her arm on one side and Heidi on the other.

"Well, a fella could get used to this."

Heidi beamed up at him. "I hear you need a suit, handsome." She placed her hand on his chest as they walked into the store. They both waved in greeting to the man that stepped from a back room.

"Hello, Rhea and Heidi. Mr. Hawkins in need of a suit?"

Rhea shook her head. "Actually no. Our friend, Conor, is after one today."

"Ah." The man's eyes lit in pleasure at the sight of a new customer. "Come inside, take a stand there on the platform please." Conor froze.

Chloe gently nudged him from behind and he stepped forward and awkwardly stood on the small box facing the girls. All stood with arms crossed and satisfied smirks as they watched him wait for the tailor to grab his chalk.

"Now, Conor, my name is Harold. I need to take some measurements and then we can try on a few styles to see which you like best and we'll fit one to you. How's that sound?"

Chloe leaned over to Rhea and whispered something and Rhea replied softly, Chloe's shoulders relaxing at her answer. Conor wondered what the two were discussing. Harold began by lifting Conor's arms out from his sides and measured his chest. He then moved to the neck and then waist. He quickly jotted down the numbers and began measuring the length of his arms. He walked behind him and measured his shoulders. Heidi wriggled her eyebrows at Conor to ease his discomfort.

"A bit nerve-racking, you all watching me."

Rhea tilted her head and smiled encouragingly. "I'm sorry for staring, Conor. It just makes me think that Claron will have to do this soon for the wedding and it makes my heart so happy. And besides, you are saving yourself from having to do this for the wedding as well. Perhaps Harold can give you a copy of your measurements and you won't have to be measured again."

"That would be grand, because I don't think I want to be. No offense, lad."

Harold waved away his concern. "You will find, Conor, that a nice fitting suit lasts a lifetime. I should not have to measure you again unless you decide to shrink or grow."

"Have you thought of what suits you want for the wedding, Rhea?" Chloe asked.

"Yes. Gray. Aunt Grace found this wonderful shop in Galway and Riley seconds it. So, I think Claron is willing to make a trip there to be fitted."

"Galway?" Conor asked. "When you have this gent here?" He pointed at Harold and the man nodded his pleasure at the recommendation. "Doesn't he handle all of Delaney's suits? Never seen a sharper dressed lad than our Delaney," Conor continued.

Rhea, feeling somewhat cornered in front of Harold, was relieved when Chloe chimed in. "Mr. Harold is good to be sure, but Rhea wishes to appease her Aunt Grace I'm sure by including her suggestions."

"Aye, I see how that's important," Conor agreed.

"Very well, Mr. Conor." Harold extended his arm towards a curtained changing room. "I'll bring you several to try. I will also bring you a button down shirt to use while you change."

Conor stepped behind the curtain. "No peeking." He heard the women chuckle as he waited. He eyed himself in the mirrored walls and shook his head. He ran a hand over his scraggy beard and wished he'd cleaned up a bit before coming to a fancy suit shop. He wasn't a man for suits. Not only were they tight and restraining against his broad shoulders, they made his burly frame seem even larger than it was. They always made him feel stuffed and unattractive. Nerves began to set in as he heard Harold returning. A shirt was shoved through the curtain and Conor made quick work of buttoning it before Harold whipped back the curtain and motioned him to stand on the platform again. Conor finished the last button and stepped out.

Heidi whistled and winked making him blush as he stumbled stepping onto the block. Rhea gently slapped her friend's arm in scolding her for embarrassing him. Harold helped slip a jacket over Conor's shoulders and it rested snug around him. The sleeves were two inches too short, but Harold told him it was just to view the style of the jacket, not the measurements. He pointed out some detail in the lapels and the girls all walked forward to survey the jacket. Heidi tilted her head and rested it on Conor's shoulder. "Too scratchy."

Rhea snickered. "Do you plan on cuddling on Conor's shoulder on *your boyfriend's* big night?"

"No, but some lucky woman might." Heidi winked at Conor again and pinched his cheek before stepping off the platform.

Chloe stood back as Rhea and Heidi circled him. Rhea finally shook her head. "Doesn't suit you." Then she giggled. "That was a pun, not intended."

Heidi shoved her back. "Nerd. But I agree. Try another one Harold."

The man helped Conor out of the jacket and quickly hung it on a rolling rack nearby. He retrieved another, a black jacket. It slipped on with ease and Conor rotated his arms a bit. Harold came around front and buttoned it closed. "This be a trim fit. Gives you a chest pocket, flap pockets, an interior pocket, and wonderful side vents." He showed each of the jacket's features. "Premium wool construction gives a classical style while the satin notched lapels," he swept a hand down the smooth lapels, "give an elegant and impressive charm to it."

"Right." Conor sounded unsure. "Not sure if a 'trim' fit is best for a guy like me."

Harold's brows rose and turned Conor towards the mirrors. "Why ever not?" He swept his hands down Conor's sides to show the fit and structured shape of the jacket, which Conor had to admit, made him look built versus stocky. "We'll give you a round." Harold pointed to the changing room and the full circle mirror display. "Check it for yourself." He nudged Conor off the platform and Conor stepped into the changing room. Harold pulled the curtains closed.

"What do you think, Conor?" Rhea's voice carried towards him.

"Aye. I think it will do." He checked the price tag on the jacket and his eyes popped out of his head. There was no way he could afford such a jacket. And he still needed to buy pants. How did a guy back out of such a situation when he had a room full of people expecting him to purchase. This was why he did not wish for an audience. He did not wish to spend an exorbitant amount on a piece of clothing he planned to only wear once.

"Alright in there, lad?" Harold called.

Conor stepped out and nodded. "Aye." He slipped out of the jacket and handed it to Harold. "'Tis a nice one."

"Yes, well if this is the one you choose, then we need to fit it to you, and then I can alter it for you."

Conor rubbed a hand over the back of his neck.

"Tell you what, I will leave it right here for a moment. Give you time to think about it while I go fetch some pants for you to try." Harold hurried off.

Chloe stepped forward. "What's the matter, Conor?" She asked quietly.

He eyed Rhea and Heidi across the room as they surveyed various suits for Rhea's wedding options should she change her mind.

Conor knew of all people, Chloe would understand his predicament.

"The jacket costs more than keeping the lights on, is what's wrong. There be no way I can justify spending that on a coat and pants."

Chloe's smile softened and her green eyes were understanding. "That be what I asked Rhea earlier. She said Harold has a company discount for employees of Delaney's."

"But I'm not an employee."

"You're better than that. You're a friend. See, Rhea told Delaney where she and Heidi were headed and he told them to have Harold put it on the company account."

"I can't have Delaney paying for my suit."

Chloe sighed. "He's not. But by putting it on his account, you receive a grand discount. Plus, the suit style itself is on sale. I checked." She tapped the side of her nose as if she sniffed out a bargain. "So not only will you be getting the sale price, but also Delaney's discount."

Conor's shoulders relaxed. "Blasted suits. Better be worth it."

"Trust me, Conor, it is. 'Twas a handsome fit for you."

Appreciative of her honesty, Conor held her kind eyes a moment longer. "Thanks for that, Chloe. And thanks for understandin'."

"Always." She smiled as Harold walked back up holding several pairs of pants. His grin turned wicked as Conor groaned at having to try them on.

«CHAPTER FIVE»

It was half past nine when Conor dropped Chloe off at her flat and neither had eaten supper due to Conor's eagerness to escape Dandy's Tailor Shop and Limerick itself. She motioned up the stairs and he followed, both happy to be back to Castlebrook. "I have a few things I can toss together." Chloe hurried to her small kitchen area as Conor stood in front of her windows overlooking the street.

"Murphy's is hopping tonight. Everyone out on a lash."

"Do you wish to go?" Chloe asked.

"No." His hands rested on his hips as he watched cars pull into Murphy's parking lot and people meander up the footpath towards the welcoming spot. "He's got a good thing going, our Murphy. No better place to have a pint than at Castlebrook's local."

"Aye, he does. Suits him well enough. Murphy needed a career that allows him to be social. He wouldn't survive not having people around to entertain."

"You have a nice view of town from up here. And you've done good work of making it feel like a home."

"Thanks." She walked towards him and handed him a glass of wine. "I don't have any beer," she added as if in apology.

He accepted the glass. "This be just fine."

She walked back towards her kitchenette and began slicing some vegetables Claron had given her a few days prior. She tossed them into a pot. When Conor turned, she was shredding meat off a roasted chicken she had leftover from the night before. "Chicken stew alright?"

"Aye. Sounds great. Thanks for feeding me."

"You've fed me plenty over the years, it's the least I can do." She smiled up at him and caught his amused stare. "What's that look?"

"Just feeling odd all of a sudden," he admitted.

"Odd? As in ill? Do you need to sit?" She hurried towards him and began fluffing the pillows on her couch and began nudging him towards it. He waved her off on a laugh.

"No. No. Stop yer fussin', lass. I'm fine." He gently tugged one of her curls. "Just seeing you at yer home is a new side of you I've never seen. I mean, I've worked in here while you're buzzin' around, but I've never seen you *living* here."

"What's that mean?"

He shook his head. "Just... 'tis nice to see you at home."

Her brow furrowed, and she shrugged. "Alright. Well, this will be a few minutes." She took her glass and walked over to one of the chairs by the windows. "I sometimes sit here and just watch the people go in and out of Murphy's. Is that stalking?" She asked on a laugh.

"Not a'tall. 'Tis good to people watch at times. Helps us feel connected when we don't necessarily want to be in all the action."

"'Tis a comfort on days I feel lonely," Chloe admitted. "Which isn't often, mind you, but it happens every now and then. And then I look down at Murphy's and see the liveliness of it and it makes me smile. Mostly I envy their energy these days."

Conor eased onto the couch again and studied her a moment. She felt his gaze on her and could see it rest upon her in the reflection of the window. Their eyes held a moment before she glanced back down at the pub. "Then it was good for you to have that rest day today. 'Tis okay to take a break every now and then."

"Says the man who doesn't."

"I did today, didn't I?"

She shook her head. "'Twas a work trip, Conor, that took you to Adare."

"Ah, but not to Limerick," he pointed out. "I did that just to appease you."

She rolled her eyes. "That is a lie, Conor McCarthy, and you know it. You needed a suit. And you found a bloody good one with the help of your friends."

"That is true. And I'm grateful for it, though I felt a bit odd trying on clothes in front of me lads' ladies."

"I'm sure Clary and Riley will forgive you this once."

"Not that I'm much competition for Clary and Riley, ay?" He chuckled, but Chloe did not smile.

"You sell yourself short, Conor. Mighty short."

His face sobered as he stood and walked over to her stew and stirred, a bit nervous now that she'd caught wind of his insecurity, no doubt. "I think it is ready."

She pointed to a row of bowls on an open shelf and he scooped them each hearty helpings and brought one over to her. He settled on the couch once more and began eating. A knock sounded on her door and had them both pausing. Curious, Chloe walked to her door and opened it. A man, tall and dark headed, a stunning face and firm build filled her doorway. Her eyes widened a bit as she opened the door further. Conor turned but remained where he was.

"May I help you?"

"Hello." He smiled, and it was just as devastating as the rest of him and Chloe felt her toes tingle. Was that possible from just a smile? "You be Chloe O'Rifcan?"

"Aye."

He extended a hand. "Quinn Kelly."

Hesitant, she shook his hand. "Nice to meet you, Mr. Kelly. May I ask what it is you need me for?"

"I was hoping for your company, lass. Your brother, Murphy, told me you were looking for a bit of fun for the evening and asked me to fetch ye."

"Did he now?" Annoyance settled over her features and Quinn's charming smile faltered a bit.

"Was he mistaken?" he asked.

"A bit. And why, pray tell, did me brother send *you* to fetch me?"

Amused, Quinn smirked as if the answer were obvious. He was handsome.

"Well, Mr. Kelly, I am sorry to have wasted your time and efforts, but I have company." She waved her hand towards Conor as he stood.

Quinn's sly grin slowly faded. "I can see that. Well, I'm sorry for it, to be sure. But a man knows when to count his losses. I will let your brother know that you are in good hands then." Gracefully, he bowed out like a gentleman though Chloe had the odd feeling he was anything but. Quinn cast one last interested glance at Chloe before meeting the hard gaze of Conor. Chloe shut the door and turned, her face flaming as nearly as red as her hair. "The nerve of that Murphy O'Rifcan to send a man to me house!" She stormed back towards her chair and stew as Conor took his seat.

"If you wish to go with the lad, I don't mind finding my leave."

"What?" Stunned, she looked up at him, her green eyes flaring. "Why would I wish to go with him?"

"Well, he's a nice-looking lad. Offering you a good time."

"Oh, he's a charmer alright, and he knows it. That Quinn Kelly is not what he seems, I'm sure of it."

"Why do you say that?"

"I could just tell," Chloe stated. "His look was disconcerting."

"I doubt Murphy would send a bad man to your door," Conor defended.

"Unless me own brother has fallen under his spell. A right faerie prince Mr. Quinn is. Dangerous, I'm guessing, in the right circumstances. We'll just find out." Chloe grabbed her phone off the end table and dialed. "You send a stranger to me door?" Her tone hinted at her mood. "Murphy Néall O'Rifcan, don't you dare be sending strange men to me house ever again." She paced. "Oh, a friend of Piper's, well that still does not make it okay. And no, I do not need a night out. I'm having a night in with Conor." She hung up and slammed the phone on the counter and then grimaced as her hand hit the edge. "Serves me right for a temper, I guess. Can you believe Murphy did such a thing? Claims Quinn is one of Piper's friends from Galway. Doesn't even know the man and sends him up me stairs." She shook her head in disgust. "Like I'm some sort of doxie, waiting for my thrills."

"I'm sure that was not our Murphy's intention," Conor added and Chloe huffed as she crossed her arms and nodded. "I know you're probably right. Embarrasses me is all. That me brother thinks I need his help in being social."

"Don't fret, Chloe. 'Twas Piper more than likely trying to help you have a fun and relaxing evening."

"By sending *that* man?" Chloe's disgust had him chuckling.

"I wager not many a woman would find such a man distasteful."

"Then they be fools. All of them." She waved her hand as if to encompass the entire non-present female population. "Because there's something off about him." She took a deep breath. "Sorry. I'll stop my ranting."

Conor grinned. "Been awhile since I've seen a Chloe O'Rifcan temper flare."

"I blame it on me tiredness. I'm feeling a bit overly sensitive."

"I can tell." He held up his hands as she flashed him a quick and direct hit with her simmering green eyes. He laughed. "Nothing wrong with it. Like you say, you're tired. Not your normal self. And it be nice to have someone to vent to every now and then."

"Aye. That's true enough. Used to be Rhea would listen to babble, but she's a bit distracted with Clary as of late."

"As she should be."

"Aye. I agree with that too," Chloe admitted, and then relaxed in a smile. "'Tis fun to see Clary so in love. Odd, but fun."

"Aye. And I agree with *that*," Conor added. "Still the same 'ol Clary but seems... better. In a way."

Chloe nodded. "Yes. As if he's blossomed a bit."

"Though I'm betting he would not like that term."

"He might." Chloe chuckled. "Blossoming is his business at times."

"True enough, but I'd say it's more yours. Has Rhea placed a big flower order for the special day?"

"Big is an understatement. Enormous is more like it. Beautiful blooms, too. A pretty penny is being spent on flowers alone. There are some that I've longed to work with but could never justify ordering. I can't wait."

"They'll be grand, I'm sure of it."

"I hope so. Have you and Riley discussed Clary's stag party yet?" She wriggled her eyebrows and he grinned.

"That'd be a no, I'm afraid. I can't seem to catch yer brother away from Heidi or Galway. When I do, we will sort it out. Clary's mentioned twice he doesn't want anything extravagant."

"That's his way." Chloe smiled. "He doesn't want anyone making a fuss over'im."

"Out of anyone, he deserves a moment of his own."

"I'm glad you think so." Chloe stood and took her bowl to the sink. "You're a good friend, Conor. Not only to Clary, but to all of us. I appreciate you letting me pal around with you today."

"I appreciate your help. With the tile and the suit." He stood from the couch and she intercepted him to take his bowl. He walked towards the door. "I best find me way home now. Long day tomorrow."

"Aye, me too. I'll be at your mam's restaurant first thing in the morning."

"I know she appreciates you filling in for me, but you don't have to."

"I know, but I'd do it for my mam too, if she needed me. You'll be back to helping her soon enough. In the meantime, I don't mind."

He walked to the door and opened it. The music from Murphy's Pub drifted up to them. He pointed at the knob. "Be sure and lock this, yeah?"

"No doubt." She smirked.

"If you don't trust Quinn Kelly, I don't either," he told her. "If you need me, call."

"I will. Thanks, Conor." She leaned against the door and he nodded for her to close it so he could witness her locking it. She did his bidding and sighed with contentment. It was nice having someone worry a bit for her, she admitted to herself. And she also felt slightly disappointed at Conor's departure. He'd always been good company. A good friend. But his presence the last couple of hours had been a change to her quiet flat. A change that felt somewhat refreshing and unexpected. She washed their bowls and laid them in the small rack next to the sink to dry and then walked back to her chair by the window. She saw Conor stopped on the footpath talking with someone, his demeanor cheerful, as always, though she knew he was exhausted. He shook the man's hand and as if he knew she looked down on him, gazed up and offered a final wave to her. She knew he couldn't see her, but she answered his wave with her own.

∞

"Clary, you have to enjoy your last night of freedom," Riley nagged, as his brother rubbed a hand over his dog, Rugby's, head. "'Tis the only time you will have before becoming Mr. O'Rifcan-Conners."

"First, there will be no hyphenating me name," Claron pointed out. "Second, 'tis not that I don't want a stag party, Riley, I just wish for it to be low key. I've spoken to Conor about it." Claron looked to his friend for support and Conor nodded.

"Aye, I had a thought on that actually."

"Well, let's hear it then." Riley waved him onward.

"Cape Clear," Conor suggested.

Claron's brows rose in thoughtfulness as Riley scowled.

"Cape Clear... where the grands live?" Riley scoffed. "No way. There be nothing to do at Cape Clear but stare at birds and drink abhorrent amounts of Nan's disgusting tea. We must party." He clenched his fists and playfully punched his brother. "Bring down the house. Celebrate. Go crazy."

Claron chuckled. "Now we know what to do for his stag night when the time comes," he told Conor.

Conor grinned.

Riley shook his head. "I can't believe you're content with just sitting idle on the last night of your bachelor days."

"I don't want to sit idle," Claron explained. "I just don't see the need to act the fool when I am happy to just hang with my mates. A pint, a pool game, and friends. That be enough for me."

"Then we might as well have it at my house," Riley stated in disgust. "If that's all you're wanting."

"Say, that's a good idea," Conor replied in earnest. "You've plenty of room for everyone. You have the upstairs for pool and darts."

"And absolutely no women would come to the outskirts of Limerick," Riley whined.

"And why do we need women?" Claron asked. "I don't want any shady business happening, Riley. I draw the line at that."

"I didn't mean—" Riley drifted off. "I just meant that it would be nice to have some females about serving drinks and treating you special. There's this great place in Galway—"

"No," Conor and Claron answered in unison and had Riley groaning.

"Piper would even back me up on it."

"I don't want Galway," Claron said.

Conor watched as Riley sank onto the bench outside of Claron's barn in defeat. "Alright. I give up. My place it is then, unless you wish to have it elsewhere."

"We could even do it here." Claron waved his hand towards his cottage. "There be no rule that we have to go somewhere."

"Here could be fun," Conor admitted. "Wouldn't have to worry about anyone having to drive to and from."

"True. But your own house, Clary?" Riley asked.

"Aye. Why not? I like it."

"And you already never leave."

"Because I like it," Claron repeated emphatically.

Sighing, Riley stood again. "Fine. Here it is, then. But you can bet we are bringing a load from Murphy's, and we will have all food catered for the entire weekend."

"Sounds fine with me."

"And have Buddy or Da take care of the cows because you are not working on stag weekend."

Claron laughed and held up his hands in forfeit. "Deal."

"And Conor," Riley looked to their friend. "We have to somehow convince the females that they are not allowed to interrupt our weekend."

"Easier said than done." Conor laughed. "Will be hard enough to separate Clary and Rhea, but to pull Layla and Chloe away as well..." He tsked his tongue.

"Aye. Agreed. That's why we need to hint at them having Rhea's getaway on the same weekend. I'll talk to Heidi and see what she says." Riley pulled out his cell phone and dialed his girlfriend. He pressed a button and put her on speaker phone. Heidi's Texan accent fluttered flirtatiously through the phone. "Well, hey there handsome. I was just thinkin' about you."

"Careful love, there be witnesses to our conversation," Riley teased.

"Oh, is that so?" Heidi chuckled. "I'm glad you stopped me."

Riley flushed a bit as he cleared his throat. "Clary and Conor."

"Oh, well hi there, boys."

"Hello, Heidi," they chimed.

"To what do I owe the pleasure of three good lookin' guys calling me in the middle of a work day?"

"To beg of your assistance," Riley told her.

"Interesting…" Heidi's sly smirk could be heard through the phone. "I like where this is going. Go on."

"Easy, love." Riley chuckled. "We're plannin' Clary's stag party and all."

"Stag? Oh, right… Bachelor party," she amended. "Stag party, got it. Continue."

"We were hoping you could sort of guide the scheduling for Rhea's towards the weekend after the museum gala."

"Hmmm…. That would put us in Galway two weekends in a row," she said.

"Galway? That's where you girls plan on having Rhea's weekend?"

"Yes. Aunt Grace is giving us run of her townhouse and obviously her name to use to get into all the fancy places in the city."

"I see."

"But I don't see a problem with the timing."

"Good. We are having Clary's party here at the cottage at the Gap and don't want female interference."

"So mysterious," Heidi jested. "You boys better not get him into trouble."

"Never," Riley swore and had her laughing.

"I'll run it by Rhea tonight and let you know."

"Thanks, love."

"No problem. Now take me off speaker phone."

Riley grinned and obeyed, taking a few cautious steps away from his brother and Conor as his conversation continued in hushed tones.

Claron rolled his eyes but smiled as he looked to Conor. "I hear you rescued Chloe from a day of boredom yesterday."

"Aye. Adare and back."

"Good. She's not one to sit twiddling her thumbs. I'm glad she could feel useful but also get away for a few hours."

Conor nodded. "She helped me find a suit for the gala."

"Did she now?"

"As did Rhea and Heidi. We stopped in Limerick and I had the whole flock clucking over me."

Claron laughed. "Better you than me. I have yet to think of suits and Rhea's about boxed me ears for not taking care of it."

"You nervous?" Conor asked.

Reflecting a moment, Claron shook his head. "Not about marrying Rhea. The wedding... a bit." He grinned. "Not sure how I feel about everyone staring at me at the end of the aisle."

"Trust me, they'll be staring at Rhea." Conor slapped Claron on the shoulder and laughed heartily.

"Oh, I'm sure. Still just a bit nervous she'll back out."

"Why would she?"

Claron shrugged. "Too good to be true, I guess."

Conor's face sobered as he looked Claron in the face. "You deserve every happiness, Clary. As does Rhea. There never be a more perfect match for you. You have nothing to worry about. Rhea loves you more than the sun."

"She must if she's choosing to live in Ireland." Claron pointed to the cloudy sky and smirked. "But thanks. Guess I'm just a bit nervous with all the changes coming about. Marriage. The cottage. Family."

"You'll have a brilliant set up here once the cottage is finished. You already do," Conor corrected, "But it will definitely be stunning once the remodel is finished."

"All we need is a neighbor." He pointed to the pasture down the slope where Conor's childhood home sat vacant and worn. "Given any thought to the property? Or can I finally buy it from you?"

Conor pulled a face and Claron held up his hands. "Just letting you know my offer is still on the table for that fertile soil you're sittin' on."

"As if I need remindin'," Conor laughed. "You remind me every time you see me."

"Just hate seeing it go to waste."

"'Tis not a waste. The fairies make use of it in the spring with their pretty flowers."

Claron narrowed his gaze at Conor and had the redhead laughing. "I have plans for it, if that's what you mean."

"Good." Claron turned to an approaching Riley. "Well, is it sorted?"

"She'll let us know." Riley pocketed his phone. "And I have dinner plans." He grinned. "Which means I need to go to O'Malley's for the messages because my house is empty."

"Cooking for the lass, are ye?" Conor asked. "Definitely serious." He winked towards Claron as Riley shrugged.

"Don't believe I'm the only one cooking for a lass these days. I was at Murphy's last night when Quinn Kelly came back to the pub feeling dejected by our little sister."

Conor's face flushed for absolutely no reason, which frustrated him. He had nothing to hide. Nothing happened between Chloe and himself.

"Quinn Kelly? Who's that?" Claron asked.

"Oh, a handsome rogue from Galway. One of Piper's friends. Seems our Chloe turned him down for a night of fun last night."

"And why is that a big deal?" Claron looked between his brother and Conor.

"Because, brother, it would seem our sister had other company last night. At her flat." Riley nodded towards Conor and he shifted uneasy under their curious stares.

"We'd just gotten back from Adare," Conor reported. "We hadn't eaten, and Chloe made a stew. That's it. Quinn Kelly shows up at her door, asks her to join him. She says no, and then goes into a temper that Murphy would send a strange man to her door. That is all."

"Kelly told a different story," Riley said with a smug smile as he crossed his arms. "Said he could feel the tension in the room, like he'd interrupted something."

Claron's brows rose as he turned to face his friend.

Conor blanched. "That be a grand lie then. I was eating. Sitting on the sofa. And I left not five minutes after the lad." His cheeks flamed, and his burly chest puffed out as he drew back his shoulders and stood to his feet.

Riley laughed and placed a calming hand on Conor's shoulder. "Cool your jets, Conor. Just a bit of teasing. Though I was a bit surprised to see Kelly come back empty-handed."

"Perhaps he chose the wrong sister," Claron suggested. "Sounds like he'd be more Layla's type than Chloe's."

"Ah, but Layla isn't finished with Delaney just yet."

"Nor will she be, I wager," Claron added. "'Tis a bit disconcerting that Murphy would send someone he barely knew to Chloe's flat."

"He trusts Piper, as do I."

"Well, Chloe didn't trust Quinn," Conor told them.

"Interesting." Riley stroked his neatly trimmed beard and then shrugged. "Oh well. At least you two had a day of it. 'Twas probably good for the both of you to travel outside Castlebrook, even if it was for just a day. Now, if only we could convince this one." He nodded towards Claron, but his brother just shook his head.

"I'm rooted." He chuckled as Riley looked heavenward.

"Don't we know it. Well, I best be heading to O'Malley's before heading home. Need to think of a grand feast for my gorgeous Rustler."

"Do you not work?" Conor asked and had Claron laughing.

Riley jovially slapped Conor's shoulder and gave him a bit of shake. "I have people for that." He winked to annoy them both, all knowing Riley worked just as hard as they did. But he whistled as if he had zero cares in the world on his way towards his truck. He tossed a final wave towards them as he headed towards town.

"Quinn Kelly," Claron repeated the name, logging it into his memory. "I'll keep him on me radar."

"Aye. He is definitely on mine," Conor admitted. "Don't like the way he looked at Chloe, nor the way he made her feel."

"I appreciate you being there."

"Right place at the right time, for certain," Conor agreed. "But Chloe's got a good head on her shoulders. She's a wise one."

"Always has been, despite being the youngest." Claron stood and walked towards the cottage, Conor falling into step beside him.

"Rhea's mam coming tomorrow?"

"Aye. She'll be staying at Mam's mostly, when she's not with Rhea." Claron bent down to grab the stick Rugby nudged against his calf. Giving it a toss, both men watched as the brown dog soared through the green grass to fetch it. Instead of bringing it back to Claron, the dog settled on the porch and began to gnaw on it. "They'll be dress shopping on Friday, I'm told."

"That's a big step in the process." Conor gave a low whistle.

Claron chuckled. "I don't even see the point really. Rhea looks beautiful in anything, and I'd marry her in a pair of denims and t-shirt."

Conor slid his hands into his pockets as they neared Claron's porch. "Aye, but that's not what a woman dreams of, Clary. She wishes to be stunning on the big day."

"Speaking of big days," Claron began. "You going to Riley's big day? Or night, I should say. The gala?"

"Aye." Conor saw the dread on Claron's face. "You not?"

"Oh, I will. Just dreading it a bit is all."

"Why's that?"

"'Tis Galway."

Grinning, Conor nodded. "I'm not a fan of the city myself, but best to be there for Riley. Plus, it is not every day you'll get to see me in a suit."

Claron laughed. "Aye, true enough." He extended his hand and Conor shook it.

"Have a care, Clary." Conor walked towards his lorry and waited two counts before turning the engine another round. It took three more tries before the engine fired up and he shifted into reverse.

"Need to let me look at that soon," Claron called from his front steps.

Conor waved in acknowledgement as he turned to head back towards his mam's restaurant.

When he'd reached the parking spot behind the building, Chloe's red hair caught his eye as she slipped out to the dumpster and tossed a load of garbage. She hurried back inside through the back door. *A busy bee*, he thought, as he shifted into park. He saw her hurry out with two large boxes and stepped in her path to intercept them. Surprise, had her jumping back on a squeal, and the boxes landed at their feet, littering the ground with shards of glass.

«CHAPTER SIX»

"Conor, you scared me!" She held a hand to her heart and bent to her knees to try and gather what glass she could with her hands.

"Sorry about that. Thought I'd help, but seems I've just made the work double."

"'Tis alright." Chloe heaved a tired sigh as she stood to her feet. "I'll fetch a broom and bin." She hurried inside and was back within seconds. Conor grabbed several large pieces of glass and tossed them into the bin while Chloe swept the scattered shards into a pile. Conor hissed and had Chloe rushing towards him. "Cut yourself?" she asked.

He held his hand to his mouth for a moment and then eyed the gash. "Nothing serious." He continued working, but she could see the gash bothered him. "Come inside, your mam has some ointment and bandages." She dumped the bin into the dumpster and walked back into the restaurant's kitchen. Mrs. McCarthy glanced up and then smiled in welcome at her only son. "Haven't seen you around in so long I'd almost forgotten your face there, boyo." She laughed at her own joke and frowned when she saw Chloe gently grab his hand and hold it under the water faucet. "What happened?" she asked, concerned.

"Just a scratch, Mam," Conor called to her. "Nothing a wee bit of ointment won't fix."

Chloe released her hold on his wrist and reached for a fresh towel. She dried his hand and then rubbed a bit of cream onto the gash. His hands were covered in calluses, scratches, and scars, and his hands seemed larger than any she'd ever encountered. *How had she never noticed that?* Conor was a big man, not the tallest of the lot when it came to her brothers, but broad and stout and a bit of a stocky giant. She smiled to herself at that thought. She guessed it made sense that a giant would have large hands. But despite their rough exterior, they wore an artist's hands. A craftsman. The roughened palms created delicate carvings and smooth finishes and quite simply, exquisitely beautiful work. She realized she'd just massaged cream into his entire hand and awkwardly dropped it. That she'd lingered over a hand, much less Conor's hand, had her taking a step back for a quick reality check. She caught an amused gleam in Mrs. McCarthy's eye as the older woman turned back to her work. A bell on the front counter had Chloe hustling to wash her hands to pass through the doors and into the dining hall. "Bandage on the counter," she called over her shoulder as she stepped through the door.

Roland, Rhea's grandfather, stood with a pleased smile at the sight of her, and her shoulder's relaxed. "If it is not my favorite O'Rifcan." He winked at her and she immediately wrapped her arms around his neck in a gentle hug.

"And if it's not me favorite American."

He laughed. "Not much competition in these parts."

"Ah, I should have added 'in the world' to the end of that then." Chloe waved a hand towards his usual spot near the front. "What brings you by? 'Tis a bit late for lunch."

Roland straightened his glasses as he propped his cane against the table. "I was hoping to speak with Conor. He's a hard man to track down these days with all his various projects. I was hoping he was here."

"He is. Or was. Let me see if he's still back there." Chloe hopped to her feet and darted back into the kitchen. Conor stood one foot inside and one foot outside the back door, finishing his conversation with his mother.

"Oh no you don't, Conor McCarthy. Not yet. You have a guest wishing to speak to you in the dining hall."

"A guest?" Conor's brows rose. "Who?"

"Our dear Roland." She saw Conor's shoulders relax as he closed the door and walked with Chloe back towards the dining hall and to Roland. When he spotted the elderly gentleman, his face split into a welcoming smile.

"Roland," he greeted, shaking hands with the man. Chloe slid into the seat next to Roland as Conor sat across from them. "Chloe here says you needed me."

"I do, Conor. I was hoping to talk with you about Rhea's wedding."

"Alright."

"Now, I know you're busy and if you don't have the time to work it in, I completely understand, alright?"

Conor eyed him curiously. "Alright."

"I was hoping you could put together an arch."

"Arch?"

"For the wedding. For Claron and Rhea to stand under during the ceremony. See, Rhea's always wanted to be married under an arch draped in flowers," Roland eyed Chloe for her opinion as well. "And well, I was hoping to make that happen. Now, again, I know you have a lot on your plate."

"Shouldn't be a problem. Arches aren't that complicated. Unless you're wanting it carved."

"Oh no." Roland shook his head. "Nothing extravagant. Just something to have as a center point for their ceremony. And Chloe, I know Rhea has given you a flower order, whatever costs need to be added to make sure flowers cover the arch, just let me know."

"I can do that." She smiled. "Will be beautiful having an arch of flowers at the top of Angel's Gap."

"Aye. For certain," Conor agreed.

Roland leaned back in his seat and smiled at the two of them. "I knew I could count on you two. So, tell me, what's been going on in the life of Conor?"

Conor just shrugged and Chloe rolled her eyes. "Making brilliant stools for Layla, he is."

"Ah, I saw them at her shop. Very beautiful work."

"You'd think so," Chloe continued.

Roland frowned. "Did something happen?"

Conor waved Chloe down. "Chloe's a bit out of sorts that Layla asked me to add tile to them."

"Ah, I see. Well, they were certainly beautiful without the tile, but I'm sure they'll be even prettier with it."

"Completely pointless, if you ask me." Chloe crossed her arms. The bell above the door jingled and she hopped to her feet and escorted the new customers to a table and supplied them with drinks. She was back within a blink.

"What'd I miss?"

The two men chuckled.

"A breath," Conor told her.

"And you two plan on attending Riley's Gala?"

They nodded and Roland beamed in pride. "Good."

"Will you?" Chloe asked. "Because I'll certainly need a handsome man to dance and dine with."

Roland chuckled and squeezed her hand. "Sadly, I will not be attending. These old bones aren't up for long car rides these days."

Concern had Chloe and Conor giving him a thorough once over and Roland sensed it. "Now, don't get worked up over nothing," he told them. "I'm fine. I just don't see myself being agile from a long trip and night of frolicking around Galway. I save that for the young folks like yourselves."

"You will be missed." Chloe leaned her head on his shoulder and Roland winked at Conor across from him.

"You flatter me, dear."

"Well, have you at least eaten lunch, Roland?" Conor asked.

"I have. Sidna saw to me earlier. Though I will be back over there for the family meal this evening. Will you be coming tonight, Chloe?"

She nodded. "Aye. I'm afraid my absence last night only made Mam worry more. She's called me three times today."

Roland patted her hand. "I will see you there then. You two have things to do besides entertain an old man." He nodded his thanks as he stood from his chair and Conor handed him his cane. "It warms my heart daily that Rhea has such wonderful friends and family here. I thank you both for being a part of her life."

"She makes it an easy job," Conor told him.

Roland's smile turned tender. "That she does." He lightly tapped Chloe's chin with his finger. "Don't work too hard, sunshine."

Chloe lightly kissed his cheek as he left and both she and Conor watched as he strolled his way up the footpath towards his flat. "A good man, that Roland." She looked up at Conor and saw his agreement.

"I best speak to Mam once more before I leave. You done for the afternoon here?" he asked.

"Aye. Was just about to head to me shop. I have two arrangements to fluff before pick up at five." She removed the apron she wore and followed him towards the kitchen. His mother glanced up and smiled.

"Roland on his way?" she asked.

"Aye." Conor gave her a brief kiss on her cheek and she snatched his chin in her hand before he could walk away. "Conor McCarthy that beard is looking a fright. Take care of it, or your mammy will."

Chloe laughed from the small room off the kitchen where she gathered her purse.

"And grab a bit to fetch some pepper. My supply does not arrive until tomorrow and I'm afraid I've about used up what's in the jar." Doireann pointed to the small ceramic bowl on the counter.

"Alright." Conor opened the till and his hand paused above the bills. "What's all this?" He held up a stack of paychecks and Doireann just shook her head in dismay.

"Ask that one." She nodded towards Chloe. "Refuses to let me pay her."

Conor glanced towards an aloof Chloe as she bent to tie her shoe. "Chloe." His voice had her glancing up. He held up the stack of payments.

She shrugged.

"Why have you not been accepting pay for your work here?"

Sighing, she glanced at her watch. "Because I don't need to. I don't mind helpin' your mam when she needs it."

"But you've been helping her for two months, lass."

"I keep my tips."

"Not the same," Conor scolded. "You will take these and cash them." He held them out to her and she shook her head.

Conor's cheeks flared and Chloe braced herself for what was sure to be a temper. "Chloe O'Rifcan, you will take the pay for the work you've done. 'Tis only right."

"I wasn't helping for pay," she challenged, taking a step closer to him, her shoulders pulled back, and chin tilted up to look him eye to eye. Doireann watched them closely.

"And we appreciate your help, but we pay our employees." Conor held them out to her again and she avoided them. "Chloe." His voice carried a warning. "Take them."

"I told you, no. You would do the same for my mam if she needed it, and I know you wouldn't charge a single euro. Only fair I do the same for yours."

"I said, take it. We don't want charity. We appreciate your help, but only if you accept payment. Otherwise, consider this your last shift."

"Conor—" His mother gasped behind him and he turned to face her.

"No. 'Tis not right for us to take hours and hours of her time and not compensate her, Mam. And I won't have it."

Chloe fisted her hands on her hips. "You can't stop me from helping."

"I can. And I will. This is just as much my restaurant as it is my mam's. If I'd known this was happening, I would have put a stop to it sooner. If you wish to continue helping, then you must work for a wage."

Chloe cast a thoughtful look towards Doireann. "A couple of coins would be fine."

"A couple of—" Conor pinched the bridge of his nose and Chloe knew he was fighting back his patience. If he wanted to haggle over compensation, she would. She did not wish for Mrs. McCarthy to pay her a full wage. The McCarthy's were family. And family helped family, with or without compensation. "Then you're done," he told her. "Thank you for helping Mam, but I'll see to that now. Now go. See to your shop."

Baffled, Chloe's mouth dropped open. "Are you kicking me out?"

"Aye." He pointed towards the door, the checks fisted in his other hand.

She huffed a bit and then snatched the checks from his hand. "Fine. I'll take the bloody checks." Storming towards the door, she turned before exiting. "But I won't be cashin' them, Conor, and that is that."

The sunshine and fresh air hit her flushed face and helped ease her frustration. She glanced down at the checks. She didn't need the money, that was the truth. She lived a quaint and quiet lifestyle that didn't require much. And though the extra income would be helpful, especially for the purchase of the nice dresses she'd be needing soon, she wouldn't dare cash the checks. On principle. She meant to be of help to Doireann, not an employee. And if she had to face off against Conor again about working at his restaurant, she'd do so. Because though she knew he hated the thought of her working for free, he also knew his mam needed the help. Help he could not provide at the moment. She heard the door open and hurried around the corner, knowing it was Conor headed to O'Malley's for his mother's pepper. The last thing she wanted was to argue with him more, but he surprised her and came around the corner instead of heading his truck. She squealed in shock as he appeared, and her presence had him jumping back a full step before he gathered his full breath.

"Bloody Mary." He held a hand to his heart. "I thought you'd be long gone by now."

"I was thinking."

"Well, I see that, lass. About gave me a heart attack."

She grinned.

"And I don't like that smug smile on your face. Makes me think you wouldn't mind doin' just that."

"I could think of several harmful things I'd like to do to you right now, if I'm being honest."

His brows rose at her abruptness. "Dat so?"

"Conor," she began. "I only want to help, and I feel by taking these checks that my help is... cheapened in some way."

Understanding crossed his face, but he still would not take them back. "I'm glad for it, your help and your heart, Chloe. But it just wouldn't be fair to accept the amount of work you've given without some sort of payment." He nudged her hand back towards her. "Consider it a bit of help to go towards all the fancy parties and wedding festivities you have coming up."

"I did think of that." She blushed at admitting the money would help.

"Then there 'ya go now."

She slid them into her purse, still unsure, but slowly coming around. "You're a right eejit when you want to be," she mouthed.

His hearty laugh had a smile breaking out over her face. "You wouldn't be the first to say so. Now go. Don't you have petals to tend to?"

"Aye."

He started to walk off and Chloe heard the cheerful tune he whistled, a Conor McCarthy rendition of Wild Rover carried in the wind from his retreating figure and made her smile once again.

∞

Conor's afternoon went by quickly as he swept the last of the wood shavings into a pile and bent to scoop them up in a dust pan to dump into the bin. It was amazing how much work he could accomplish when he wasn't interrupted. He'd finished the serving pieces for Sidna that Mr. O'Rifcan had requested for their upcoming anniversary. Sidna was one of his best customers when it came to serving pieces, and he was glad to add more to her collection. He'd laid the patterns for Layla's stools. The blue and white tiles created a floral mosaic that he thought she'd find enchanting. He hoped. Tomorrow he'd mix the grout and begin laying the first one. He swiped a hand over his sweaty brow and reminded himself to talk to Mr. O'Malley about the air conditioning. The lack of air was not much of an issue on sunny days when he could raise the windows. But on cloudy, muggy days when the skies swelled with restrained moisture, he could not open the windows for fear the humidity would affect the wood in his shop. And it made for sweltering working conditions that had him dripping sweat by the end of the day.

He put the broom in the small closet in the back corner and then flicked the light switch off. Locking up, he stepped onto the footpath and locked his door. He spotted Chloe and Layla doing the same at their own shop, the two sisters conversing quietly, their voices a gentle hum on the breeze that began to pick up as the next Irish storm began to blow in. Layla's thick brown hair whooshed across her face, and even in annoyance and against Mother Nature, her movements were graceful when swiping it out of her eyes. Chloe's ringlets looked like flames of a fire, sporadic in movement and whipping to and fro. Both women were beauties in their own right. Conor had to admit he'd loved the O'Rifcan women from the moment he met them, Sidna included. All possessed qualities he hoped one day he'd find in a lass of his own.

Layla spotted him and sent him a wave causing Chloe to turn and do the same. "Best be on your way home now, Conor," Layla called. "We're about to have a slosher."

"Aye. You lasses need a ride to the B&B?"

They shook their head, but a large splash of water landed on the back of his hand. When he looked up, the skies unleashed their burden and all three of them ran towards Conor's truck. Layla hopped inside and sat in the middle seat between Conor and Chloe. The smell of floral and vanilla mixed with the smell of sawdust and wet skin as they crowded into the confined space.

""Thanks for the rescue." Layla patted his arm as he tried to start the engine. It sputtered and died. He cranked again and it did the same. He growled.

"Of all times for it to give up." Layla shook her head in dismay. "Looks like we'll have to leg it, Chloe."

"Now, wait a minute," Conor told them. "Let me give her one last try." He did, and nothing. Silently, he berated himself for not having taken the time or Claron's offer of help to fix the truck's issues. And now he had to send two of his most favorite people running through a storm.

Chloe opened the door and quickly hopped out, followed by Layla. Both women began to sprint up the footpath. It wasn't long before he could hear them squealing and splashing one another from the puddles they encountered. He was glad they were in good spirits despite his failure to keep them dry. He on the other hand, felt like an oaf. He lowered his head to the steering wheel and sighed.

A tap sounded on his window and he found a smiling Murphy on the other side, hunkered down beneath a rain slicker. "Need a rescue there, Conor?"

Conor hopped out of his truck and over into Murphy's. "Bloody possers to boot." He hated wet socks, especially when they settled into wet boots.

Murphy shut his door and flipped back his hood. "Might as well come to the meal." He tapped his watch.

"Like this?" Conor waved a hand over his stained shirt and sweaty appearance. "Your mam would have me hide showing up in such a state."

"She values a hardworking man," Murphy told him. "As do most women. Right there, Jeanie?" He called over his shoulder.

Conor froze and turned in surprise to find Jeanie Connors sitting elegantly in the back seat, her luggage surrounding her.

"Hi there, Conor. Good to see you."

His face flushed in embarrassment as he extended his hand to her. Her small-boned hand felt like a kitten's paw as he clumsily shook it. "Didn't realize Murphy had company. Good to see you, Mrs. Connors. Thought you were expected in town tomorrow?"

"I came early." She held a finger to her lips as her eyes sparkled. "I wanted to surprise Rhea. I was also just too excited. I can't wait to start helping with wedding plans."

"A great surprise," Murphy assured her.

"I'm thankful Murphy here came to my rescue and picked me up at the airport."

"'Twas my pleasure, Jeanie." He beamed, his flirtatious smile not only reserved for those his own age, but for any pretty face. And Jeanie

Connors was a striking image of a gracefully-aged Rhea. She flushed, as do all females when Murphy O'Rifcan turns a glad eye.

"Sorry Paul couldn't make it just yet," Murphy continued.

"Oh, he is just beside himself with jealousy," she chuckled. "He loved it here when we came for the proposal. I imagine once he wraps up things with his retirement, he'll be here within a day."

"We'll win you both over to Castlebrook before long." Murphy winked in his rearview mirror and she grinned.

"Well, if Claron and Rhea have babies, you can bet that will only add to its charm." She sighed happily thinking of grandchildren.

"You and Mam can pray together on that one," Murphy told her. "Though I wouldn't hold me breath. Mam's been praying for more grands for several years, but her children have yet to acquiesce."

"It's only a matter of time," Jeanie assured him. "I can't wait to see all of you happily married off and families growing."

Murphy whistled under his breath. "Give me time, Jeanie," he teased.

She laughed and then looked to Conor. "Do you have someone special, Conor?"

"That would be a no," he told her. "Not at the moment."

"Though that not be the word around the village," Murphy baited.

Conor narrowed his eyes at his friend. "And who's doing is that, Murphy?"

"I haven't spread any rumors, Conor McCarthy, if that's what you're implying. I was simply there when your whereabouts were discussed."

"Now this sounds intriguing." Jeanie leaned forward in interest, her hands clasped above her knees as she cornered Conor with what could only be described as the 'mom stare.'

He groaned and had the other two laughing. "A friend was feeding me and the entire village goes haywire," he told her.

"Not just a friend. My little sister," Murphy countered.

"Layla? But I thought she was with Delaney?" Jeanie asked.

"Not our Layla. Our Chloe," Murphy explained. "A late night supper for our Conor and Chloe at Chloe's flat."

"You're making it sound like way more than it was. 'Twas two friends eating together. Nothing more." Grinding his teeth to hold off on scolding Murphy further, Conor eyed the cars parked along the street in front of the B&B. Murphy found his place and hopped out, sheltering Jeanie with an umbrella. Conor hoofed it to the porch and opened the bright red door as Rhea's mother swept inside like a breath of fresh air to a room full of surprised faces.

«CHAPTER SEVEN»

"Jeanie?" Sidna stepped forward and wrapped Rhea's mother in one of her famous bone-crushing hugs. "Look at you blowin' in with the storm. The Connors' way it seems." Sidna hit Roland on the shoulder as he sat in his usual arm chair. He stood and Jeanie walked into his arms and gave him a kiss on the cheek as they embraced.

Senior O'Rifcan nudged his way through the room, which wasn't hard as everyone moved out of his way so as not to be crushed. He lifted Jeanie off her feet as he kissed her cheeks. "So happy you've made it, Jeanie."

She laughed as he set her back on her heels. "Thank you. Feels wonderful to be here." Her eyes found Claron and she walked towards him in pure excitement as she hugged him close. Her hands tenderly brushed over his hair as she framed his face with her hands. "Hi, honey." She kissed his cheek. "Rhea in the city tonight?"

He nodded and she released his face and squeezed his hand. "Well, she wasn't expecting me until tomorrow. That will give me time to rest. But first, what is that heavenly smell, Sidna?"

Sidna straightened in pride. "Lorena's got supper on the table." She waved everyone to the dining room and chairs clattered as they all sat. Chloe watched as Jeanie took Rhea's usual seat by Clary and was pleased to find her brother completely comfortable in the woman's presence. Her eyes met Jeanie's and the woman beamed. "Ready to dress shop, Chloe?" She rubbed her hands together in anticipation.

Chloe nodded. "Aye. We've been flipping through books for weeks."

"Oh, I'm so glad Rhea has you girls here to get excited with her. How is Heidi? And Layla? Is Layla joining us?"

At the sound of her name, Layla breezed into the dining hall, a satisfied smirk on her face. Her eyes adjusted to the sight of Jeanie and she gasped. She reached across the table and squeezed the woman's hand. "I was about to box Clary's ears for bringin' another woman to the table, but I see he's safe."

Jeanie chuckled. "This poor boy could never escape Rhea now, no matter how hard he tried."

Claron smiled.

"Not that he would want to," Murphy chimed in. "Our Clary be the lucky one in this relationship. If he hadn't snatched your Rhea up, one of us brothers would have." Several of the other men nodded their heads and Jeanie grinned.

"And a fine lot to choose from," Roland complimented. "Speaking of relationships, Tommy how is Denise?"

The redheaded O'Rifcan brother swiped a napkin over his mouth before responding with a simple, "Grand."

Footsteps sounded in the sitting room and Aine and Declan whooshed in on a wave of rain, both shedding their coats. "Hello to the house," Declan called, he and his wife making it into the dining hall just as Conor came in, freshly washed. Chloe's brows rose at the sight of him.

"Oh, right," Murphy announced. "I invited Conor."

Sidna stood and bustled Declan and Aine to seats and then nudged Conor further into the room and pointed to the vacant seat next to Chloe. "So glad you could join us, Conor." Sidna kissed the top of his head as she walked down the side of the table and did the same in welcome to Aine and Declan. Declan still wore his Garda uniform and Aine her scrubs, but both looked relaxed and happy to be with family.

"No Riley tonight?" Declan asked.

"No. He is entertaining his lass tonight. Cooking and all."

"'Tis the 'and all' part that sounds more intriguing," Murphy teased and had some of the brothers chuckling. Sidna swatted him behind the head on the way to her chair.

"An important time for our Riley and Heidi. They deserve an evening together before hectic festivities distract them," Layla reported.

"We're surprised to see your face at the table too," Murphy told her.

Layla smiled. "Well, Delaney has a late night of it at work, something about preparing training sessions for tomorrow, and he sounded bloody exhausted."

"Could have taken him a meal," Murphy replied. "Given him a break."

"Trust me brother, if I had taken him a meal, there would have been no break." She winked at him and had him and his other brothers groaning at her implication."

"Layla Aideen," Sidna scolded. "No such talk at the table."

Layla only grinned and winked towards Chloe, as if sisters approved of such conversations no matter the circumstances.

"Is everyone attending Riley's gala?" Jeanie asked.

Most nodded their heads.

"He was so sweet to invite Paul and me. I bought a special dress for it. Though I won't have Paul with me."

"I'll dance with you, love." Murphy reached for her hand and kissed the back of it. Jeanie blushed though she playfully swatted away his charm.

"I imagine you will have your hands full, Murphy, being the charmer you are."

"Jace and Jaron will be there as well," Sidna told her. "Or at least I've told them to be."

"I believe Jaron plans to," Murphy said. "Haven't talked to Jace."

"Those boys have been scarce," Senior interjected. "Either they have secret lasses or have shunned us."

"My bet is on the lass part," Declan replied.

Sidna's eyes sparkled. "Oh, I do hope so."

Claron chuckled at his mother. "Easy, Mam."

"Oh, posh." She winked at him. "A mammy can wish for all her children to be happy and loved, can she not?"

"Absolutely," Jeanie agreed.

Sidna waved her hand toward Jeanie in a sweeping gesture as if the woman's agreement solidified her case.

"All my little ducklings starting to find their way and their matches makes a mammy's heart want to burst."

"Not all of us," Murphy corrected. "Chloe and I are holding out, right little sister?"

Chloe looked up from her meal and forced a smile as she chewed her food.

"'Tis only a matter of time," Sidna continued. "And our Conor, of course."

Chloe heard Conor choke on his sip of water and she bit back a laugh.

Her comment was all the fuel Murphy needed to tease Conor and Chloe once more. "Perhaps you're right, Mam. If the town gossip is correct, we'll see another match soon enough."

Sidna's brow furrowed as if trying to decipher what her son was talking about, but Chloe shot him a warning glance and Murphy winked at her. *Infuriating man,* she thought.

"And how is our Piper?" Senior asked Murphy. "She moving to Castlebrook yet?"

Murphy shook his head in disappointment. "Not yet. Blasted woman still thinks life in Galway is better. And with Riley hiring her for his gala, she's only rubbed that in me face any chance she gets."

Senior's bellowing laugh brought smiles to everyone's faces. "Hang in there, boyo. A hard-headed woman is worth the effort. Piper will come around."

"Perhaps if you wooed her," Sidna told him.

"I want her to work, Mam, not date me," Murphy clarified.

"Well, why not both?" Sidna asked.

Murphy just rolled his eyes and shook his head. "Because I don't want a bloody lass, I want help at the pub. And if me efforts don't pay off soon with Piper, then I'll extend my search in Limerick instead. The woman is trying my patience."

"Good things come to those who wait," Layla told him. "Just look at Delaney and me."

"And you were just *waiting* for him, were you?" Murphy's sarcastic response had Claron biting back a laugh as Layla's eyes sparked at both of them.

"He was a nice surprise," Layla continued, unphased. "But I didn't wait around to pursue him, now did I? I jumped at the opportunity."

"Our Mr. Hawkins had no chance after that," Senior roared as he slapped his knee.

"No, he did not." Layla flicked her hair over her shoulder and smiled proudly.

"Yes, well, I'm different. I'd like to take my time," Murphy continued. "Like Clary did."

"That boyo was lost the moment his eyes landed on our Rhea," Senior pointed out. "Just took him time to feel brave."

"I am sitting right here," Claron remarked and received an encouraging pat on the arm from

Jeanie. "But 'tis true enough that Rhea bewitched me from the start."

"The one that got away." Murphy clenched his fist to his chest and feigned a look of longing on his face before his lips broke into an amused smile and laugh.

"'Tis hard being second fiddle, isn't it brother?" Claron teased, his chest puffing proudly as he settled back against his chair.

Murphy's mouth fell open as Chloe burst into a surprised laugh at Claron's jesting.

"Second fiddle, he says?" Murphy's eyes gleamed.

"I would like to note that I was not second fiddle with Renee O'Callen back in the day." He looked at all his brothers and they grinned.

Declan's laugh echoed down the table. "Renee O'Callen. Of all women, that's the one he chooses to bait us."

The other brothers laughed as well.

"You can have your Renee, brother." Declan grimaced. "Did you see her last winter when she came to visit her grands?"

"Declan," Aine scolded.

"Just saying," he continued. "I'm glad I lost on that one."

Murphy bent his head in shame and everyone laughed.

"And if that's the last lass that's caught yer eye, I'd say we have bigger issues," Tommy teased.

"Oh, now that's not right." Murphy laughed.

"I think this talk needs to be shelved before it gets too out of hand," Sidna warned.

All the boys sobered and ate their supper quietly.

"So Chloe," Jeanie began. "Rhea tells me she's given you her flower list."

Chloe nodded. "Yes'm. I plan to buy some sample stems next week to put together some test arrangements for her to choose from as well as what she'd like to use for her bridal portraits."

Jeanie smiled. "I cannot wait to see. Where do you find your flowers?"

"A wholesaler in Shannon, mostly. There may be a few I have to retrieve in Galway, but I think I can gather the bulk of them in Shannon."

"How wonderful." Jeanie sliced a piece of the juicy beef tenderloin on her plate.

"What day you going, sister?" Layla asked.

"In a week or so... once Rhea finds her dress and we can envision a bouquet to match."

Layla pouted. "Shame. I will be working on new potions at the shop. Was going to offer to ride with you, but one of us will need to be at the store."

"Aye," Chloe agreed.

"Be careful," Aine warned. "The traffic has been awful towards Shannon lately." Aine, a nurse at the hospital in Shannon traveled the highways every day and sometimes night, and Chloe nodded at her warning.

"How be my stools, Conor?" Layla asked.

"Coming along," he replied.

"And brilliant," Chloe added.

Conor eyed her with an amused smirk, her constant need to defend his skill to Layla made him grin.

"Oh, to be sure," Layla said. "I can't wait to see them."

Chloe finished her meal and stood. Her mother eyed her with interest. "I'll plate the desserts."

Sidna nodded and waved her on. When she reached the kitchen, she relaxed. Claron followed in behind her and had her startling in surprise.

"Escaping, sister?"

"A bit."

"You seem out of sorts." Claron set about fetching fresh bottles of wine to pair with the pies their mother had baked.

"Layla just getting under me skin."

"About the stools?"

"Aye. I think it selfish on her part to keep demanding changes to what is beautiful workmanship already. 'Tis not fair to Conor to keep making them a priority when he has a fair share of other projects he needs to work on."

"Isn't the decision ultimately his, though?" Claron asked. "I'm sure if Conor did not have the time, he'd let Layla know."

"I doubt it. 'Tis Layla. Every man jumps at her bidding."

Claron's right brow rose at the subtle bitter tone in Chloe's words. His youngest sister was never one for a spoilt attitude. "I don't think Conor falls for Layla's charms. He's just being a good friend."

Sighing, Chloe plated the first slice of pie. "I know you're right. I'm overreacting. I'm not quite sure why it bothers me so."

Claron hid his smile as he uncorked the first bottle. He poured a glass and handed it to her. Chloe took a calming sip. "Thanks. How are you?"

"Good."

"Overwhelmed yet?"

"In a grand way."

She smiled tenderly at him. "I'm beyond happy for you, Clary. Truly."

He flushed as he set the bottle in a basket to carry them into the sitting room. "Thanks." In typical Claron fashion, he diverted the attention off himself and nodded towards the door. "We best prep the room for the others or Mam will have our heads."

Nodding, Chloe gathered the plates of pie and walked into the sitting room.

∞

Conor accepted the dish from Chloe as he made his way into the cozy room full of worn couches and crowded tables. Despite the close quarters, everyone found a spot and enjoyed the dessert Sidna had prepared.

Claron stood next to him by the mantle and took a bite of his pie. He started to mumble something when Conor's cell phone rang. He quickly answered it, walking towards the stairwell to speak in private. "Hey Mam," he greeted.

"And where are you this evening?"

"The B&B. Murphy kidnapped me."

"Ah. Well, that's well and good then. You could have let a mammy know. I was keeping a plate warm for ye."

"Sorry, Mam." He pinched the bridge of his nose. He knew his mam valued their evenings together and by eating with Chloe the night before and currently at the B&B, he'd forgotten to see about his mother.

"Don't be apologizing. There be no need, boyo. Makes a mammy happy you're spending more time with friends. Make it up to me by sharing a coffee in the mornin'."

"Will do. Have a care." He hung up and pocketed his phone.

"You being summoned?" Claron asked quietly.

"No. Mam just wasn't sure what'd become of me. She's not used to me actually having a social life these days."

Claron chuckled. "I understand that."

And of all his friends, Conor knew Claron definitely understood. "Doesn't help matters I'm all she has. Needs to find her a lad, Mam does."

"And you'd want that for her?" Claron asked.

"Of course, I would. She's been on her own since I was a wee lad. She deserves her own happiness. And any man that would make her feel special would be fine in my book."

"Perhaps one day then."

"One day," Conor agreed.

Chloe walked up and quietly joined their conversation. "You best intervene, Clary, or Murphy will have an entire evening planned out for him and Jeanie."

"Hitting on her, is he?" Conor's brows rose.

"Not quite, but in a way. The scoundrel." They all smiled knowing Murphy had no intentions of interfering with Jeanie and Paul Connors' marriage, but their charming brother aimed to make her feel welcome and special, and he would, if need be, treat her to a nice meal and evening out.

Claron stepped towards Jeanie and sat next to her, his presence welcome as Jeanie reached over and squeezed his hand. "If Clary ever wondered what Rhea would look like in thirty years, he has his picture," Conor remarked.

"Aye. She's marvelously beautiful." Chloe's small sigh had him turning and he realized her gaze was not on Jeanie and Claron, but she was affectionately watching Declan and Aine whisper to one another, their arms linked and heads bowed in private conversation.

"They be planning something, you think?" he asked, nodding in the direction of the O'Rifcan brother.

"Not sure. Something secretive is definitely going on between the two," Chloe admitted. "We shall see. I'm going to head home. I'm a bit tired after today and from the sprint."

"Sorry about me lorry. Hate that you and Layla had to drown."

"No worries." She patted his arm. "'Twas good to stretch our legs a bit. I'll be seeing you, Conor."

"Aye. Night."

She said her goodbyes to her parents, lingered over Roland a moment as she always tended to give him special attention, and then went on her way. Conor contemplated his own exit but he caught Senior's eye and the man beckoned him for a game of chess. And since he'd not made the time to visit with the man over the last few weeks, he easily complied knowing the next hour would be spent losing gracefully.

«CHAPTER EIGHT»

Chloe hurried towards her door, grabbing a light scarf on her way and hastened down her steps to the awaiting car. Only it wasn't Layla's car sitting in front of her flat, but instead a shiny black limousine. She froze a moment until a goofy grin spread over her face. The driver stepped out, tipped his hat, and opened the back door. Chloe poked her head inside.

"Chloe!" Rhea's cheerful tone called to her from across the car. "Get inside! Hurry! We still have to pick up your mom."

"What on Earth is this?" Chloe slid inside and accepted the champagne flute Jeanie handed her, a crisp mimosa with a cherry on top.

CHLOE

"Aunt Grace sent it. We are making the rounds, picking everyone up, and then we're off to the dress shops in Galway where Layla and Aunt Grace have made appointments."

"This be so fancy." Chloe giggled with the rest of them. "Where be Layla?"

"She ran into the store right quick and will be back." At Rhea's words, the door opened, and Layla slid inside with a bag full of her creams and lotions. "For Aunt Grace. She texted me a last-minute order."

Rhea's smile radiated through the car as pure happiness seeped from her every pore. The limo made its way up the streets of Castlebrook and to everyone's delight, every single person it passed, stared.

"Not every day such a car travels the roads of the village." Chloe watched the red door of the B&B swing open as Claron stepped out carrying a large bouquet of flowers he'd had Chloe prep the day before. Rhea gasped as she scurried from one end of the limo to the door. She crawled out and ran towards him. He swooped her into a hug and swung her around, the two sharing a show-stopping kiss on the front lawn. Rhea's gaze traveled over his shoulder and she gasped. "Aibreean?" Rhea rushed towards Claron's grandmother and enveloped her in a tight hug.

Sidna linked arms with Nan and helped her down the stairs.

Rhea then returned to Claron's side and accepted her flowers. "She wished to join in on the fun," Claron whispered.

"Did you drive all the way to Cape Clear to bring her here?"

"Aye."

Rhea kissed him again before letting him nuzzle his nose in her neck.

"There be plenty of time for that after the wedding!" Heidi yelled from the open skylight of the limo. "Rhea, get your booty back in the car and let's go!"

Chuckling, Rhea hugged him one last time as Chloe helped her grandmother into the car. When all the ladies had found their places, Rhea switched places with Heidi and stuck her upper body out of the skylight. "I love you, Claron O'Rifcan!" She blew him an excited kiss and waved goodbye.

Chloe watched as her brother's handsome face exploded into a glowing smile before he lightly dabbed a knuckle near his eye. She squinted to study him and caught his joyful watery gaze through the window, though he couldn't see her through the tinted glass. His happy tears made Chloe's eyes water as well, but she sniffed them back as Rhea slid back into her seat and accepted her champagne glass from Heidi.

"I'm so excited I could scream." Rhea laughed as nervous energy had her shaking her hands in front of her.

"Pretty sure you just did," Layla teased. "The entire village heard you confess your love."

"Good," Rhea nodded. "I want everyone to know how I feel about Claron."

"Does a Mammy's heart good to hear such talk." Sidna beamed as Nan relaxed against the seat beside her.

"I'm so glad you came, Aibreann." Rhea reached forward and clasped her hand.

"I wouldn't miss it, me love. I knew you were Clary's the moment he brought you to me house. I'm glad you both grew wise to the idea."

Rhea grinned. "But what about Aodhán? He's not alone at Cape Clear, is he?"

"Oh heavens no." Aibreann laughed. "Dat man will be getting his hands dirty today, yes he will. He and Clary have a big day planned."

"Good." Rhea sighed happily as she leaned back against her seat and sipped on her mimosa.

Chloe's phone dinged with a message and she reached into her purse. A photo. She opened the text and eyed the picture Conor had sent her. It was the mosaic on the top of Layla's stool. He then sent another photo of the stool as a whole.

Chloe: "A beauty."

Conor: "You think Layla will like it?"

Chloe: "She'd be a grand fool not to."

Conor: "Good. I'll take them by tomorrow. How's the car? Heard you lasses squealin' across the way."

Chloe: "Beyond amazing. Feel quite fancy ridin' about."

Conor: "As you should. Enjoy your day of celebrating."

Chloe: "Thanks. Wish me luck on finding a dress."

Conor: "No luck needed. You'll be a beauty no matter what."

She paused, and her heart skipped. *Did Conor just call her beautiful?* She rested the phone in her lap a moment and stared out the window as they passed hedgerows of blackthorn and lush green fields. *Odd*, she thought, *how her heart had reacted to such a comment.* He was more than likely being kind. *But what if,* she thought. *What if Conor was meaning to be sweet to her? What then? What did that mean?* Did she care for Conor? *Of course.* But did she care for him as more than a friend? And if so, when did that transition happen? She couldn't recall. But somewhere, deep down she felt a light tug in her heart at the idea of him thinking her beautiful. And she hoped that she would find a dress that would confirm his compliment.

"Earth to Chloe." Layla tossed a grape her direction and she caught it before it landed on the seat.

"What did I miss?"

"Rhea's rule," Layla answered, pointing at Chloe's cell phone. "There be no working today. Just time with friends, meant to be enjoyed."

"I'm not working," she told them. "I was—" She paused. "'Twas a friend."

"Well, shelve that conversation for a minute." Heidi clinked her glass with a pen. "I think we need to toast this gorgeous woman beside me." She held her glass towards Rhea and all the women raised their own. "To the kindest, most loving, and sort of the nerdiest woman, I've ever known."

Rhea laughed at that and clinked her glass with Heidi's and then towards the middle with everyone else's.

"No better lass for our family," Sidna added.

"No better friend to us all," Chloe continued.

"And no better love for our Clary," Aibreann ended.

Jeanie lightly dabbed her eyes with a white handkerchief and Rhea gripped her hand.

"You O'Rifcans make it easy to love you," Rhea told them. "Though don't tell Murphy I said that."

Sidna hooted in laughter and had everyone doing the same.

By the time they pulled up to Aunt Grace's townhome, Chloe had consumed three mimosas, and she was trailing behind the rest of the women. All were full of giddy smiles and funny stories. And when Aunt Grace slid into the car leopard-print high heels first, her blood red fingernails wrapped around two more bottles of champagne, the giggles erupted once more.

∞

It was just a text, Conor reminded himself. Yes, she hadn't responded since, but she was busy. Perhaps she didn't read too much into it. Yes, he meant it. Chloe was beautiful. Always had been. Always would be. And he was sure that no matter what dress she ended up finding, it would indeed look stunning on her. *But why did he tell her that? And why, for heaven's sake, was he still thinking about it? About her?*

He *knew* why.

He'd watched her float down her steps and stop in sheer shock of seeing a limousine outside her door. The pure excitement that had radiated from her smile had stopped him dead in his tracks on his way to his shop. He'd never seen her smile like that. The wonder of it all... to be pampered so for the day. And he had no doubt Rhea's Aunt Grace would indeed pamper all the women. The woman had money to burn and she viewed Rhea as her own. They'd be off trying on gowns, having their hair done, their nails, their makeup. Well, he wasn't sure if they were doing *all* of that, but it painted a pretty picture in his mind, so he stuck with it. Smiling to himself at the mental picture, he wasn't aware of Murphy O'Rifcan's presence until he'd all but bumped into the man.

"A bit distracted, are we?" Murphy eyed him suspiciously.

"Apologies, lad." Conor straightened, leaning his weight on the broomstick in his hands. "What brings you by my shop?"

"I'm here to kidnap you... again."

"Whatever for?"

"A rooster gatherin' at Clary's."

"A what?" Conor rested a hand on his hip as Murphy laughed.

"All the women are off having a grand time for the day, so we men should do the same. Riley's on his way back from Galway, Declan, Jace, Jaron, and Tommy are already at the Gap. Roland is on his way, and if we can peel Delaney away from his office, he'll be coming too. And I am grabbing you to carry with me since your lorry is still down and out."

"Sounds like a family gatherin'," Conor replied.

"And?" Murphy crossed his arms and leaned against the counter as Conor rested his broom against the wall. "You be family."

The inclusion the O'Rifcan family gave Conor always touched him, but he also never wanted to intrude on the off chance there were moments meant to be shared only amongst the brothers.

"Clary asked me to grab you, now are you coming, or do you plan to keep sweeping?"

Knowing Claron wished for him to be there, Conor nodded. "I'll come. Can't say I have a drink to bring, but if we run by me—"

Murphy pointed at himself. "You're riding with me, Conor. Remember? You won't be needing drinks. I've all the drinks a man could ever want. They're currently growing warm in the back of me truck. Now come along."

Murphy waited patiently for Conor to lock up and then drove in his usual careless manner as they made their way to Angel's Gap. There was smoke rising from the back porch and the smell of roasting meat had Conor's stomach growling, though it was still several hours from lunch time.

"We drink. We throw meat on a grill. We lurk about outside... this is what men do," Murphy recited as they walked up to find the other brothers sitting or standing about the porch. Declan tossed Conor a bottle of beer and then one to Murphy.

"Find your way, did you?" Tommy took a long sip of his drink. "When are you going to give up on that lorry, Conor?"

"Never."

"'Twas afraid you would say that," Tommy laughed. "Mr. O'Malley is near tired of it sitting in front of the market."

"It'll be moved soon enough."

"When Clary fixes it," Jaron added.

Conor shrugged. "Not in me plans to buy a new vehicle any time soon. Plenty of other things to take care of first, so it will sit until I've time to tinker with it."

An engine roared up the road and the top of Riley's truck could be seen coming up the drive.

"Seems Riley's made it after all." Declan reached into the cooler beneath him and fetched his brother a beer. As soon as Riley stepped onto the porch, on instinct he caught the bottle midair and popped the top.

"What have I missed?"

"Absolutely nothing," Jace told him. "Tom is nagging Conor about his truck, Clary's daydreamin' but pretending to pay attention, and Dec's on his third bottle."

Riley clinked his with Declan's in a toast. "Sounds like my kind of party. Passed the ladies on their way to Galway."

Claron perked up at that news, and Conor found himself intrigued as well.

"And?" Claron asked.

"And what? I waved. Heidi popped out of the top to blow me a kiss and made several cars swerve and fear for their lives just like any gorgeous siren would." He beamed proudly. "And off they went."

Claron's shoulders fell.

"Are you seriously sad to be missing out on dress shopping?" Riley asked on a laugh.

"Not a'tall," Claron replied. "Just missing the love of me life. Is that a crime?"

His brothers groaned in unison and Murphy shook his head in dismay. "Is this what you've become, Clary? Love-sick? Though you saw Rhea not but an hour ago?"

Claron held a hand over his heart and smiled. "'Tis a blessing and a curse to have such a lass."

Declan chuckled. "Aye. Once you find the right one, there's no turning back. Aine can still look at me with those soft blue eyes and make me melt. I'll forever love that about her."

Murphy stood to his feet. "Bunch of saps, the lot of ye." He walked towards Claron's back door, disappearing inside and coming back out with a bag of crisps. "Lasses be the death of you, if you're not careful." He crunched and then offered the bag to Jace who retrieved a handful of crisps for himself.

"I like to live dangerously," Riley admitted. "'Tis why I chose Rustler. No better catch than that one. Full of fire and curves. *So* many curves." He grinned wickedly as several of the brothers smirked.

"And Denise," Tommy began and then widened his eyes. "When I hold her... she fits just right. You know? Never had that before."

"Mush," Murphy continued to banter.

"Don't be so hard on them, brother," Jace laughed. "Your time will come."

"As will yours," Murphy pointed out. His jaw dropped when Jace's cheeks reddened at his comment. "Wait... have you a lass, Jace?"

Jace leaned back against the railing and a sly grin spread over his face. "There's this lass in Shannon—"

Murphy groaned and held his hands to the sides of his face. "Conor and I be the only ones of sound mind these days. What's the world coming to? The men in me family are fallin' like pawns in a chess match against Roland."

"And happily," Claron added.

"Well, I guess it is up to you and me, Conor. We should go out on the lash and leave these shmucks behind."

Conor shook his head and took a sip of his beer. "I be fine right here."

Murphy's eyes narrowed as he studied their friend. "And why is that?" he challenged. "Don't tell me you have a secret lass now, do you?"

"No. I just happen to like the smell of what Clary's cookin'."

The brothers laughed and toasted towards Conor in agreement, as Murphy settled himself back into his chair and brooded over the crushing turn of events in his brothers' love lives.

Conor felt his phone buzz in his pocket. His grin slowly faded as he studied the picture Chloe had sent him. The women were trying on dresses, and Chloe's picture was of herself dressed in a soft pink number that made her look like a fairy queen in his opinion. He was surprised she'd send him a picture, but before he could type a response another message had come through.

Chloe: "Pink is definitely not me color. Yikes."

Not her color? Baffled, he responded.

Conor: "Not sure if we're looking at the same picture... you look whimsical."

She didn't respond, and he wondered if his compliment was, once again, a bit forward. But when he stared at the photo a moment longer, he felt a twinge in his chest. When he scrolled to zoom in on her face, her familiar smile softened him. He wasn't quite sure what had changed about Chloe's smile, perhaps nothing, but the way it was making him feel was definitely different. *Why?* he wondered. He felt a jab against his elbow and Claron cast him a curious and questioning gaze. Conor cleared his throat and shoved his phone back in his pocket, making a strong effort to focus on time with the lads instead of Chloe O'Rifcan's beautiful face.

∞

Layla spun in a full circle in front of the mirrored wall before her as the other women sat on plush sofas and chairs. "I do like the color." Layla glanced over her shoulder to peer into the mirrors behind her and frowned. "Not a fan of the fit."

"I think it looks lovely, dear," Sidna told her.

Heidi shook her head. "A bit schoolmarm-ish."

Layla nodded in agreement as Rhea laughed. "It's beautiful, Layla. Anything you wear will be beautiful, but if you aren't comfortable in it, try a different style.

The sales woman ushered over another dress and Layla's eyes sparkled. "Now this be more Heidi's flavor, I believe." She ran her finger over the low-cut neckline and Heidi shimmied in her seat with a grin. "If you got it, flaunt it," Heidi cheered.

Aunt Grace hooted in laughter as she reached for a strawberry on the center table. "You girls just make my heart sing."

Jeanie and Rhea shared a smile as Layla hurried behind the curtain to the left. Chloe stepped out of the fitting room on the right in a light sage green dress that swept over one shoulder and trailed in a train in the back. The chiffon fabric added a touch of elegance and breathiness as she stepped on the platform.

Rhea squealed as she hopped to her feet and immediately began turning Chloe in circles. "*Love* this color on you, Chloe. I think this one is yours, but I'm not sure I like the one shoulder drape."

"Me either," Chloe agreed. "But the color is nice."

"Yes, makes your eyes pop." She and Rhea grinned into the mirror as they both surveyed the dress. "I think you should try one with a halter neck. You have great shoulders and could pull it off." Rhea looked to the attendant and she buzzed to the back of the store and returned with Rhea's request. Chloe obediently stepped off the platform.

The curtain to the left whooshed open and Layla struck a pose. "Look out lasses, for Layla O'Rifcan has come to make a statement." She flipped her leg out and the long seductive slit in the dress showcased her lean, tan leg. She gave it a flirtatious kick as she danced her way to the platform in a lavender dress that fit her like a glove.

"Heidi, eat your heart out love." Layla wriggled her bosom towards the Texan and stuck out her tongue. "For this one be mine after all."

Aibreean whistled and the women all laughed. "'Tis a brave woman to wear such a thing."

"Aren't you wanting to keep a little mystery about you, sister?" Chloe asked.

Layla circled on the platform. "Whatever for? I have me a lad. A mighty handsome one at that. And my Mr. Hawkins will be drooling like a fool when he sees me in this."

Rhea shook her head on a laugh. "Then it's done. If you love it, I love it. Heidi, you're up."

Heidi hopped to her feet and went to the rack housing pale pink dresses. She nudged hangers until her hand froze and she pulled one out. "Alright, here goes nothin'." She hopped into the fitting room Layla had just vacated as Layla stepped to the side to be fitted. Though there was little to be done other than hem the bottom of the dress.

Chloe slipped back into her dressing room and slipped into the new dress. When she zipped the back and fluffed her hair over her shoulders, she knew she'd found the one. Rhea was right. The halter neck style elongated her neck and somehow made her shoulders seem more graceful. She ran her hand down the soft fabric, the same chiffon as the previous dress, but yet fitted and flowy against her slim frame. She stepped out and Jeanie gasped.

"Oh Chloe." Her reaction had the other women looking up and Sidna beamed.

"Me little one." She stood and walked towards Chloe and kissed her cheek. "Absolutely lovely."

Rhea nodded, her eyes serious. "You look gorgeous. How am I going to compare to my amazing wedding party?" she laughed.

Chloe did a slow twirl for them to see the back as well.

"Do you like it?" Aunt Grace asked.

Chloe nodded. "Never felt so pretty or worn something so fine." She squeezed Rhea's hand before she reached for the tag to check the price. Her eyes briefly widened at the cost.

Aunt Grace, noticing the color drain from Chloe's face, stood to her feet. "I have an announcement to make." She clapped her hands. "Heidi poke your head out, dear. Layla, you listening?" She turned to find Layla glancing their direction. "Now I know Rhea's dress is a gift from Jeanie and Paul, but I would like to purchase all of the gowns for the wedding party, including Sidna, Aibreean, and Jeanie."

Jeanie's jaw dropped. "Grace, you don't—"

"No. I want to." She beamed at Rhea as she embraced her. "Part of my gift to Rhea."

"Part?" Rhea's eyes widened. "Aunt Grace, this is enough. Thank you."

"Oh no, sweetie." She winked. "I've got a couple other things up my sleeve."

Rhea just shook her head and hugged her again. Aunt Grace reached for Chloe's hand and gave it a reassuring squeeze. "That is your dress, Chloe. Absolutely stunning."

"Thank you." Chloe hugged her. "And thank you for purchasing it."

Aunt Grace waved away her thanks as her eyes grew teary. "Now, Heidi, get out here so we can see what damage you're going to do to the male population."

Wriggling her brows, Heidi flipped the curtains back and stepped out in an elegant flash of pink, the simple A-line cut not what anyone would have thought the bold Texan would have chosen. The modest cut did nothing to hide the incredible figure lurking beneath but instead, enhanced it.

Rhea covered her mouth as Heidi did the mandatory circle of observation. "Heidi, it's beautiful. You look beautiful. Once Riley sees you in this, we may end up having a double wedding."

Heidi burst into laughter. "That will be the day. I still have a while yet before I tack that man's boot to the floor."

Aibreean and Sidna chuckled, knowing full well Heidi was right in her assessment.

"But it will at least make his heart stammer, and that's good enough for me."

"No man is safe with the lot of ye." Aibreean shifted on the cushion as she spoke, her small frame appearing even tinier amongst the plush cushions. "And dat is how it should be."

"And what of you, Nan?" Layla eased onto the sofa next to her grandmother and lightly brushed a hand over her soft white hair. "What will you be wearing to make Grandda swoon?"

Aibreean's soft smile blossomed like a young woman in love. "I have in me mind what I'm lookin' for. We shall see if I find it. But your Grandda will lose his head, he will. But first," She looked to Rhea. "What of our bride?"

Aunt Grace stood and clapped her hands for attention. "Yes, it is Rhea's turn next. I have us lined up at the most wonderful bridal boutique a few blocks over. They are expecting us in a few minutes. So, let's get the bridesmaids' dresses purchased and packaged, unless they're needing alterations. In that case, I can bring them to Castlebrook in a couple of weeks for the bridal portraits."

Chloe hated to take off the lovely dress. She felt Rhea tug on her arm and pull her towards the center of the mirrored platform and slipped her arm around her waist. Aunt Grace and Jeanie stood poised holding their phones to take a photo.

"Such beauties." Sidna swiped a tear from her eye and Jeanie reached over and held her hand, her own gaze softening.

"Stop your blubbering, Mam." Layla waved a hand in front of her own face. "Or you'll make the rest of us a mess."

The women wrapped their arms around one another in a large group hug until they all began to laugh. "I think it's time for a wee tipple in dat fancy car." Aibreean shouldered her purse and led the way outside. Sidna walked with her and Jeanie to the car as the younger women changed out of their dresses and Aunt Grace handled payment. Rhea shot a text to Claron as Chloe watched her green dress be bagged. Aunt Grace handed it to her with a wink before turning and grabbing Heidi's dress from the rack.

Rhea's phone dinged almost instantly. She nibbled on her bottom lip as she started to smile.

"You sending love notes to me brother?" Chloe asked.

"I sent him the photo of you guys in your dresses."

"Ah. And what does Clary have to say?"

"Said he wants to frame it."

"Oh, that brother of mine." Chloe grinned as Rhea read another message that came through. "Said all the men are trying to fight him for his phone to have a peek."

Chloe rolled her eyes. "No sneaking him photos of you in your dress, though."

"I hope I find one. Aunt Grace went through all this trouble of lining up the shops."

"You will." Chloe encouraged. "I've got a good feeling. And we're off to a good start, no?"

"True. I am amazed you all found dresses so quickly."

"So, see? Perhaps our luck will carry over."

"You have to be brutally honest with me, Chloe." Rhea began. "If I try on a dress and it does not look good, no matter how much I may like it, you have to tell me it's a no."

Chloe chuckled. "You forget we have Layla and Heidi with us. I have a feeling they will vocalize their opinion for you."

"Yes, but I want yours. You and I have similar tastes," Rhea explained quietly. "I don't want to... well... flaunt, so to speak. I want Claron to think me elegant."

Chloe wrapped her arm around Rhea's waist and pulled her in for a hug. "He will. I promise."

"Thanks."

"Now let's go before Nan drives away on her own."

Laughing, they left the boutique arm in arm.

«CHAPTER NINE»

Aodhán and Claron Senior walked towards the cottage, the younger men and Roland still relaxing on the back porch, as the setting sun cast warm hues of orange and red over the cliffs of Angel's Gap. Conor watched as Aodhán paused at the edge of the porch and stared out over the landscape, no doubt remembering his time living in that very spot. Claron walked up to his grandfather, draped an arm around his shoulders and murmured something to him that had a soft smile spreading over the man's face before he patted his grandson on the back and turned to walk towards one of the rocking chairs Riley vacated for him. On a sigh, the old man sat.

A car door shut and a voice carrying a phone conversation drifted towards them as a disheveled Delaney made it to the edge of the porch. He motioned that he'd be a moment longer before venturing further towards them.

"That man never knows when to stop working." Jaron shook his head. "Don't know how Layla stands it."

"Don't be hard on the man," Senior bellowed. "He be a good fit for our Layla. Serious. Strong-willed. Those be qualities she needs."

"Aye. True enough. But just looking at the man makes me exhausted. He and Clary both, in different ways."

Senior smiled and slapped his son on the back as he greeted Murphy by shoving his feet off the railing to walk past him. "Have we heard from the females?"

"Clary received a right pretty picture a bit ago." Jace motioned for Claron to show their dad. He obliged and Senior grinned.

"Not a bad sight, now is it?"

"Not for me." Riley's smile was mischievous and had his father chuckling.

"Best show it to Delaney, but may want to wait until he's finished with that phone call first,"

Senior joked, his robust laugh making his sons grin. "Conor, glad to see you, boyo." He shook Conor's hand before patting him on the shoulder in welcome. "Still can't fathom why you'd want to hang around with this lot." He laughed at his own joke as he watched Claron open the grill cover. "Then again, maybe I do." Claron flipped several pieces of meat and then closed the cover again, and in a collective sigh of resignation, all the men relaxed back into their chairs.

Delaney walked up the porch, slipping his phone into his slacks pocket. "Sorry about that." Declan handed him a beer and Delaney politely took it but not before Riley let out a snort.

"Dec, keep your beer. Our Mr. Delaney likes his whiskey. Am I right?" Riley motioned to Murphy who sat on the top of a cooler, the bartending brother obliging by reaching into a crate by his feet and pulling out a half-finished bottle of Jameson. He poured two fingers worth into a plastic cup and passed it towards Delaney.

Delaney nodded his thanks.

"Looks like you need it," Murphy observed.

"Busy day is all." Delaney knocked back the glass and Riley held his phone in front of the man so he could see the picture of their women in their dresses. Delaney choked on his sip when he spotted Layla and had all the men laughing as Riley pounded him on the back.

"Take your time, lad." He handed Delaney his phone and watched as the man zoomed in on Layla.

"Wow." His lack of words had the men laughing again. "Didn't even know they made dresses like that. They all look lovely."

"Lovely?" Riley eyed him in disdain. "Drink some more of that and then tell me this picture is just 'lovely.'" He chuckled as he passed the phone to his grandfather who then passed it to Conor who had yet to see the picture. Again, his eyes gravitated towards Chloe, and he felt similar to Delaney. He quickly handed the phone back to Riley so as not to draw notice.

"And is there a final suit we be wearin', Clary?" Declan asked.

Claron sighed as he rubbed a hand over the back of his neck. "I'm sure there is, but I haven't been told yet."

Murphy laughed. "Rhea doesn't trust you to pick one out?"

"I wish to wear whatever she wants us to."

"Speaking of suits," Delaney looked to Conor. "Was Dandy's able to help you out, Conor?"

All eyes fell on him and he nodded. "Aye."

"And what suit you be buying?" Riley's brow rose.

"For your gala," Conor told him. "Need to look me best for all the women of Galway." He rubbed a hand down his robust chest and had his friends laughing.

"Aye. As you all should. There be plenty of them."

"Then I guess they are all for Conor and myself." Murphy grinned. "Seeing as how all of you gentleman have lasses already." He toasted towards Conor. "I feel it will be a good night for us, Conor, my friend."

Shaking his head on a laugh, Conor toasted back. "Perhaps so."

"Have you seen me girlfriend?" Riley asked them. "Why would I need to feel bereaved of such foolishness? I've got the most beautiful one there."

"Minus Rhea," Claron pointed out.

"And Aine," Declan added.

"And—" Tommy started but was shushed by an annoyed Riley.

"Alright, we are all lucky. I get it. Let me have my moment. I have a beautiful lass. Let me bask."

Aodhán laughed at that. "We all know I have the beauty. No mistaking Aibreean is me heart's match. Aon duine níos áille."

"He loses me when he does that," Conor whispered to Claron.

"Said there be no one more beautiful than Nan," Claron interpreted.

"Ah." Conor played those words over in his mind and found he liked the sound of them. He knew some of the old language, but not enough to carry on a conversation like Claron. And Aodhán floated between English and Irish constantly, making the old man hard to decipher at times. But like all the O'Rifcans, Claron's grands were some of the finest people he knew. Aodhán had been good to Conor as a boy when he lived down the hill, and when he and Nan moved to Cape Clear, Conor felt almost as sad as Claron. In some ways, the O'Rifcans truly were family. His life had been tied to them since his birth, he and Clary being so close in age. They'd been friends since they were babes. And when Conor's da had up and left his mam, it was the O'Rifcan family who tended to them, Senior stepping into the role of father figure, and Aodhán as well, until they moved. And all the siblings welcomed Conor into the fold throughout the years. Murphy, with his friendly disposition, treated him like a younger brother. Riley as well, but more of a friend. Conor cleared his throat, as the sudden wave of emotion hitting him surprised him. He eyed the beer in his hand and tossed it into the bin. *Enough of that,* he thought, thinking the dark liquid was toying with his emotions.

Claron eyed him suspiciously, keeping his comments to himself, but Conor noted the look of concern. "I'm fine."

"Never seen you toss a bottle."

"Just... lost me taste for it all of a sudden."

"You ill?" Claron smirked as he took a sip of his own beer.

Conor relaxed and laughed. "Must be, hm? Perhaps the only cure will be some of what yer hidin' in that pit there."

"Aye, perhaps for me as well. Fetch a platter. Let's feed the masses."

∞

Rhea stepped out onto the platform in a white fluff. Her dislike was evident as the attendants rushed around her to spread the dress out around her ankles. They pulled the back of the dress and clipped it to fit it to her body.

Heidi burst into laughter at the sight and everyone grinned.

"'Rhea? Rhea? Are you in there?" Layla called on a laugh as Rhea rolled her eyes.

"I think this one is a no," she told the attendants.

"What do you not like about this one, Rhea?" Chloe asked.

"You like it?" Layla turned stunned eyes on Chloe and Chloe shook her head.

"But if she knows what she does not like about it that will help dwindle down other options."

"Good thinking, Chloe." Jeanie walked towards Rhea and slipped her fingers under one of the beaded shoulder straps to feel whether they were comfortable or not.

"Well, I don't want something so... big." Rhea held her hands out around the bell-shaped bottom half of the dress.

"Alright, so no robust bottom," Layla told the boutique's attendants. "How about the top? Do you like the cut?"

Rhea's face fell in disappointment as it seemed the first dress she tried on would determine the rest.

"Don't be gloomy yet," Chloe whispered and rubbed a reassuring hand on Rhea's back. "There be plenty more to try."

"I just want something simple... with lace."

"Give me a moment." Chloe held up her finger and walked over to the boutique attendants. "Excuse me," she began in hushed tones so Rhea would not hear. Instead, she saw that Rhea was in conversation with Sidna and her mother. "Do you have anything of lace, full lace. Preferably an A-line fit. Bit of a train. Something fit for a fairy." She grinned and the women nodded and one of them darted towards the back of the shop. She returned with a white dress bag and unzipped it. Chloe's eyes sparkled as she nodded. She took the bag. "Rhea, let's try this one." She motioned for Rhea to shuffle back into the dressing room and Chloe unzipped the bag.

When she pulled out the dress, Rhea gasped. "Oh, Chloe." She covered her mouth as her other hand trailed over the lace and beadwork. "Yes... I want to try this one."

Chloe helped her out of the fluffy tulle dress and hung it outside the room. Rhea slipped into the new find and Chloe began fastening the buttons on the back. Rhea ran a hand down the front of it as the soft lace draped to the floor. She looked every part the fairy princess, Chloe thought. She found Rhea's watery gaze in the mirror, her friend nodding, speechless, as she envisioned walking down the aisle to Claron wearing such a dress.

"This be the one," Chloe smiled.

Rhea nodded. "Most definitely. How did you know?"

Chloe shrugged. "Just thought of what I could picture in me mind and asked them."

"It's perfect." Rhea hugged her. "Mom is going to cry." Rhea sniffled as she herself began to shake her hands in nervousness.

"All the women will," Chloe told her. "But good tears. For we're all so happy for you and Clary."

Rhea squeezed her hand in thanks as Chloe pulled back the curtain and Rhea stepped out. The room fell quiet as the women watched her step up onto the platform.

"Rhea—" Her mother held a hand over her heart as her eyes grew glassy. Rhea's head bobbed as in answer to Jeanie's question.

"This is it," Rhea announced.

Aunt Grace beamed as Sidna walked towards Rhea and grabbed both her hands. She kissed both her cheeks. "You be all Clary will ever want, dearie. Absolutely stunnin' in that dress."

"Thanks, Sidna." Rhea looked to Aibreean and the old woman stood, reaching into the pocket of her slacks. Rhea looked down from the platform and smiled as Aibreean opened Rhea's hand and placed a small hair pin into her palm. She closed Rhea's fingers around it. "Something old," she told her.

Rhea opened her hand and stared at the small pin with pearls and emeralds. "'Tis a gift for you, love," she said. "Me mammy had a full set of these. I wore them on me wedding day to Aodhán and every O'Rifcan bride has worn one since. Lorena pinned it to her flower bouquet. Aine wore it pinned to her veil. Sidna wore it tucked in her hair. The choice is yours whether you wish to wear it or not, but 'tis me gift to you. For you are now an O'Rifcan as well."

Rhea stepped down and enveloped the small woman in a tight embrace. "I would love to wear it. Thank you, Nan." A tear slipped down Rhea's cheek as Aunt Grace stepped forward with a dainty handkerchief. "Something borrowed." She dabbed Rhea's tears and then unfolded the small hanky to reveal intricate stitching. "This was given to me by Roland years ago when I first moved to Ireland. Sort of a good luck gift. I'd like you to use it on the big day, should you need it."

Rhea's lips quivered as she smiled and nodded.

"Something new." Jeanie walked forward, carrying a small rectangular box. She opened it and a delicate chain of diamonds sparkled in the lights.

"Mom—" Rhea tenderly touched the jewels.

"You always loved my bracelet." Jeanie held up her wrist and her own diamonds dazzled. "Now you will have your own." She took it out of the box and clasped it around Rhea's wrist and kissed her daughter's cheek.

Rhea beamed at the strong women before her. The sisters and Heidi exchanged a smirk, not going unnoticed by Rhea. "What is it? What do you three have up your sleeve?"

Layla walked a small bag over to Rhea. "We've brought yer somethin' blue."

Rhea reached into the bag and her face flushed as she pulled out the tiniest pair of sky-blue lace panties she'd ever seen.

"Oooee, now if that doesn't get Clary's wheels a-spinnin' nothin' will."

Heidi burst into laughter and grinned as the other women began to tease Rhea as well.

Rhea sobered. "Thank you all so much. If you would have asked me a year ago if all of this was possible, if this happiness was possible, I would have said no. So much has happened and changed over the last months, I feel as if I'm in a dream." Layla pinched her and Rhea flinched. "Ouch. Not literally." She playfully swatted Layla as the sister shrugged. "You are all a dream come true. I could not ask to be joining a better family. And Claron... well, he will be *so* loved, I assure you." She looked to Sidna when she spoke. "I love him so much." Her voice cracked as Sidna walked forward and embraced her.

"Aye, lass, we know, and we're forever thankful for you in return. You've made our Clary so happy." She kissed Rhea's cheek and sniffed back her own tears.

"Enough of this blubbering." Aunt Grace waved her hands through the air and grabbed the champagne glasses on the small table and began handing them out. "Now, we celebrate Rhea and Claron, and finding her perfect dress. Crying is for the birds."

Everyone laughed as the attendants began ringing celebratory bells and the sounds of cheers, bells, and clinking glass filled the room.

∞

Conor rubbed a hand over the front of his suit jacket, unbuttoning and rebuttoning, not sure which way looked best. He tugged at the collar of the crisp white button up he wore and hunched his shoulders. He straightened them back out, adding a couple more stretches to shift the suit and feel more at ease. The suit itself fit nicely, it was tailored perfectly to his body, but his gracelessness came from the fact he never wore suits. He felt stiff. Awkward. And unsure. Perhaps he'd just not go. But then guilt immediately filled his chest. He'd have to go. Riley would be disappointed if his family and friends did not show up.

He rubbed a hand over his neatly trimmed beard, which in itself was also a sight. It'd been so long since he'd tamed his face, he'd almost forgotten what he looked like underneath. He wasn't sure how he felt about it yet. He felt slightly exposed, but he had to admit it made his appearance tidier and more put together. But he also felt somewhat... nervous. It'd been years since he dressed up and attended a fancy gathering. In fact, he couldn't remember the last one. Perhaps Declan and Aine's wedding years ago. Either way, Conor McCarthy and fancy were just two things that did not go together. At least, not without some persuasion.

Sighing, he straightened his jacket one last time. It was as good as it was going to get. He fetched his keys and then groaned. His truck was still parked out front of O'Malley's with a discombobulated engine. He contemplated who he could call so as to carpool, hating that he had to. A knock sounded on his door and he stepped out of his small apartment at the back of his mam's restaurant to find his mother standing there, arms crossed waiting for him to answer.

Her eyes widened in surprise at his appearance before her eyes grew glassy. "Me boyo." She reached up and cupped his face and kissed him on both cheeks. "Might fine you look, Conor. Mighty fine. So handsome," she blubbered, brushing a hand over his jacket. "A smart suit, that is."

He blushed under the extra attention and reached for his phone. "I was on me way to Galway for Riley's big night. Did you need me for something?"

"Ah, no." She shook her head and held her hands against her cheeks as she kept studying him in pride. "Makes a mammy's heart swell to see her boyo all handsome like."

"Alright, Mam." He rolled his eyes as he brushed passed her and out onto the footpath.

"No lass be safe in Galway with the sight of you."

"Mam," he groaned but smirked at her obvious joy. She hugged him once more, the familiar scent of the restaurant clinging to her.

"Murphy called. Said he was swinging by to pick you up."

"Oh good. I was just about to call him."

"You two be careful now. Safe. Give Riley me best. And a kiss for such work."

"Well, I won't be doing that, but I'll tell him you're proud of him all the same."

She chuckled as Murphy's car swung next to them. He hopped out and whistled. "I'm here to pick up Conor McCarthy, have you seen the lad?" He smirked as Conor waved him off.

Doireann laughed. "You keep me Conor out of trouble Murphy O'Rifcan, do you hear me?"

Murphy's brows rose as he stepped on the sidewalk and twirled Conor's mother in a happy dance before dipping her and popping her back up and planting a firm kiss on her cheek. "Doireann, me love, he is in good hands with me."

"Dat is what I'm afraid of," she chuckled, even as she blushed and nudged him away. "On with ye. You two lads have fun. And BE CAREFUL!" she yelled at them as they started driving away.

Conor rolled down the window and gave her one final wave, his mother blowing a kiss before heading back inside the back of the restaurant.

They reached Galway in an hour due to Murphy's speed, and the city was thriving. They parked and due to most of the area being pedestrian walkways only, they legged it towards Eyre Square a few blocks away.

Murphy pointed to a row of buildings, and it was easy to recognize the touch of Riley O'Rifcan. The brick structure, while maintaining its historical framework, boasted a glass roof that speared into the sky with slashing awnings and diverse angles. The modern twist fit the modern art Conor knew would be inside. Riley stood at the door, a gorgeous Heidi draped on his arm as he welcomed his work crew, friends, and family. He spotted his brother and beamed. "Wondered when you'd get here." Murphy pumped his hand and pulled him into a hug.

"Proud of you, brother. Looks bangin'."

"Thanks."

Murphy leaned forward and kissed Heidi's cheek before bowing before her. "And you, Heidi love, have stolen me breath." Her laugh fluttered on the breeze as she accepted his attention with a beaming smile. "Stop it, Murph, or you'll have me in a tizzy." She winked at him as he stepped towards the door and shook hands with a few familiar faces.

Conor slapped Riley on the shoulder in greeting, the O'Rifcan brother doing a double take as he eyed his friend. "No way!" Riley pulled Conor into a friendly pat. "Who is this handsome, lad?" He eyed Conor's suit and tugged on the lapels of his jacket. "Don't look Heidi love, or you'll fall in love with him."

Heidi turned and smiled at Conor. "You do look sharp tonight, Conor. I almost didn't recognize you. I think this is the first time I've ever seen your face." She kissed his cheek and then lightly rubbed her thumb over it to erase traces of her lipstick.

He blushed and started to step towards the door but Riley caught his arm. "I want to thank you, Conor, for your work here. Already people have been inquiring of who built the bar. I hope you don't mind me passing your information along."

Baffled that his work would turn such a glad eye, Conor shook his head. "Not a'tall. Glad to do it for ye, Riley boyo."

Riley smirked and then nodded for him to continue on his way. Conor had barely stepped through the door when a waiter standing with a tray of champagne flutes offered him a tipple. He accepted, and his eyes searched the crowd of people for anyone familiar. When he spotted her, his feet planted and his heart dropped to his knees. Chloe stood in a small group, her hair pulled back in a fancy twist of some sort, a few ringlets framing her face. And draped in a sleek black dress that looked of pure silk. She wore makeup, that being a new look for her, but not overdone so as the true Chloe still shined through. Conor realized then that Chloe O'Rifcan looked right magnificent, and he would not play the fool and miss out on talking with such a beauty.

He walked towards his friends, Rhea spotting him first. Her lips lifted into a welcoming and pleased smile as she nudged Chloe. When Chloe glanced up, he saw the shock in her expression and prayed his appearance was just as pleasing to her as hers was to him.

«CHAPTER TEN»

Chloe felt her heart stop, she swore it, as Conor stepped forward. Claron greeted his best friend with a warm handshake and Rhea hugged him tightly before brushing a hand over the front of his suit and patting his arm. "Chloe," he greeted. His usual steady, blue gaze held trepidation, and she found she couldn't look away.

"Conor. Seems that suit was a good choice after all." She smiled as his face relaxed a bit and he shifted from one foot to the other. "I have you to thank for that. And Rhea and Heidi." He nodded towards an amused Rhea as her eyes bounced between the two. "You look—" His long pause caused her to hold her breath. "Captivatin'."

Her heart hammered in her chest as she felt her cheeks warm. "Thanks."

Rhea shifted slightly as she turned to talk with one of Riley's partners, her slight bump to Chloe from behind not going unnoticed by Conor. He reached out and lightly took Chloe's arm to stabilize her and she swore her arm tingled from his touch. Rhea's tiny steps as she spoke, Chloe knew, were to nudge her closer to Conor, but thankfully their dear friend seemed oblivious to Rhea's matchmaking scheme. Worse than Mammy, Chloe thought, but a faint smile had her inwardly thanking Rhea for giving them a moment of private time.

"You know anyone else here?" he asked, his eyes carrying over towards the bar. The bar he'd crafted specifically for Riley and the space. Piper's head bobbed behind the counter, the spirited blonde dressed to kill in a dashing blue number. She watched as she saw Murphy slink his way up to the bar to speak to her. She smirked when Piper acknowledged him with a clipped nod before tending to her wait staff. He was in her territory now, and Chloe hoped it would help Murphy appreciate Piper's skill even more seeing the woman in action.

"My heart has stopped and my toes have curled!" Aunt Grace's voice drifted towards them as she spotted Claron and Rhea. Her eyes then focused on

Chloe and she opened her arms for a hug. When she eyed Conor, she nuzzled up next to him and hugged him, her hand resting on his chest. "Now this is a man in a suit." She brushed her staple red nails over the front of his neatly pressed shirt and smiled up at him. Rhea bit back a grin as she looked to Chloe.

"Conor McCarthy, we need to bring you to Galway more often." Grace openly flirted as she sighed happily. "Isn't this just lovely? Riley has truly outdone himself with this project. And he told me you designed the bar, Conor. Such incredible work." She grabbed one of his hands and rubbed her finger over the calluses there. "Yes, a man who works with his hands is a fine man indeed."

"Easy, Aunt Grace," Rhea warned, chuckling at an embarrassed Conor.

"Oh now, Rhea, a woman can appreciate a handsome looking man, can't she?" Adoringly, Grace looked up at Conor again. "Especially a big, strong man."

Claron cleared his throat on a laugh as he took a sip of his champagne, casting Conor an apologetic look for Grace's advances.

"You know, Conor," Grace continued. "You should ring me up the next time you're in Galway. I have this wonderful little café down by the harbor that serves the best fish and chips." She continued fussing with his shirt collar, Conor's face growing redder by the minute.

Chloe took a small step towards them and draped her arm through Conor's. "If you will excuse us Grace, Conor and I were on our way to the bar to have a word with Piper."

"Oh yes." Grace reluctantly slid away from Conor's side and draped her arm with Claron's and began the same routine of touching and adjusting lapels and collars. "I'll just tend to Rhea's handsome farmer now." She winked at Rhea and Chloe as Claron just shook his head in defeat.

Chloe tugged Conor towards the bar.

"Thank you, lass," he whispered.

She giggled. "Grace does love a dashing man in a suit."

"A bit like a lioness, isn't she?"

"Oh aye,." Chloe agreed and they grinned at one another. "Rhea says she is all but in love with Riley."

"What lass isn't?"

"Also a bit true. Though I think the tides are shifting there thanks to Heidi's presence."

"True enough. Our Rustler would put up a mean fight if it came to it."

Laughing, Chloe waved to Piper as they approached the bar.

"Now, if it's not two of me favorite people," she beamed. "Lookin' good, Conor. Almost didn't recognize you."

"That seems to be the consensus tonight. Didn't realize I'd let meself slip so much. Put on a fresh jacket and give me face a trim and everybody loses their head." Though his voice was teasing, Chloe knew the reactions he was receiving had to be somewhat overwhelming.

"A compliment," Chloe assured him. "Though we all love the Conor we see every day as well."

Appreciatively, he looked down at her, their gazes holding. Piper nudged two glasses of champagne their direction. "Well, me beauties, enjoy your night in the city. If you need anything, just let me know."

"Chloe?" A voice had Chloe's back snapping to attention and Piper's face spread into a wide smile.

"Quinn. Quinn Kelly." The man leaned down and lightly brushed his lips against her cheek. "Remember me?"

"Aye." Chloe took a cautious step back and felt Conor's hand at the small of her back. She instantly felt protected.

"You look gorgeous." His eyes gleamed as he set his empty flute on the bar top. He winked at Piper as he reached for Chloe's hand. "Would you like to dance? They've got a small floor open over there." He pointed to an area across the room where several couples swayed to the live music that drifted towards them.

Chloe was speechless. She didn't really want to dance with Quinn, but she felt cornered. Piper nodded for her to say yes, Quinn waited expectantly, and Conor just stood silently beside her.

"Of course she would." Piper answered for her and plucked Chloe's glass out of her hand and set it on the bar. "Go. Dance with the man." She winked and Quinn grabbed Chloe's empty hand and tugged her towards the dance floor. She glanced over her shoulder to Conor, his eyes never leaving hers. She saw his shoulders stiffen, but to her disappointment, he didn't follow.

∞

"I think it a fine idea," Layla, her arms draped around Delaney, rested her chin on his shoulder and stared at him until he replied.

"I would need to check my calendar."

Delaney's usual response had her rolling her eyes, but she still gave him an intimate kiss despite the crowd around them.

Riley toasted towards him. "Done then. Just let me know and we'll get you on the list."

"A list, have you?" Layla asked. "Seems Clary's stag party will be grander than what we have planned for Rhea," she frowned.

"'Tis not an actual list, just a figure of speech, sister. But Clary's stag party will be a night to remember." He winked.

"Better not have gorgeous females hanging all over you," Heidi warned as she walked up and slid her arm through Riley's.

"Only if you're there, love." She tapped a finger to his lips and narrowed her gaze on him. "I'll pretend to believe you."

He laughed and held up a hand in honor. "I promise. No shenanigans of the female sort are planned."

"Good," Layla and Heidi replied in unison.

"Though of the whiskey sort," Riley feigned a grimace. "I can't promise that."

"Just don't jump off the cliff trying to prove you can fly," Heidi teased.

Delaney chuckled. "Now that would be a sight."

"Hadn't given the cliff much thought actually." Riley rubbed his chin. "Would definitely be fun to try something there."

"Riley," Layla warned. "You may be a fool, but my Delaney is not. If you so much as try a half-brained attempt at flying across that cliff, I'll have your head."

Riley shrugged. "'Twould be impossible anyhow, sister. Maybe..." he added, still contemplating ideas.

Conor walked up and Riley opened his mouth to share his and Delaney's brainstorming when Layla cast him a sharp glare. He modified his approach. "Conor. Having fun?"

"Aye. Lovely party, Riley."

"You lose me little sister somewhere?"

Conor motioned towards the dance floor. "Quinn Kelly asked for a spin."

"Quinn Kelly." Layla turned and eyed the man on the dance floor. "So that's the man that put her in a tizzy a couple weeks ago."

"Aye. That be the one."

"Well I can see why." Heidi took a step closer, she and Layla now facing the dance floor intrigued by the gorgeous man.

"Now, now… don't be like that." Riley tugged Heidi back to his side and Delaney just grinned as Layla's arm found its way back through his.

"Right nice to look at, isn't he?" Layla asked.

"Very nice," Heidi admitted. "Perhaps Chloe will—"

Riley cleared his throat and pointed at himself. "Older brother standing right here, love."

Heidi chuckled, grabbing his chin and giving his face a wriggle. "Fine. I'll keep that to myself."

"Thought she hated the man," Layla stated.

"Hate who? Not me, I hope." Murphy stepped forward and beamed at the group. He followed the groups' attention towards the dance floor. "Ah. Quinn Kelly. Seems Chloe was not immune to his charms after all."

"What do you know of the man, brother?"

"Not much. He's a friendly sort. Piper suggested him for Chloe."

"Suggest, did she? Thought that was just at the pub the other night." Riley's brows rose in curiosity.

"No idea. He seems nice enough," Murphy pointed out.

"Charming, I imagine, if he's convinced our Chloe to dance." Riley admitted.

"That'd be Piper's doing, I'm afraid," Conor told them. "Walked up and asked for her hand, he did. Piper made the decision for Chloe and all but put her in a spot."

"Ah. Such a shame to be forced to dance with a gorgeous man," Layla pretended to whine. She then looked at Delaney. "Though I wouldn't mind a dance with my lad." She brushed a finger down Delaney's cheek, and he blushed at the public display of affection.

"Right." He set his glass down, nudged his glasses up his nose, and swiftly tugged Layla towards the dance floor before her attentions grew too bold for his liking.

Riley laughed as Murphy took a long sip of his drink. He gurgled as a loud clap on his back had him sputtering. He quickly recovered and accepted the excited hug from his mother and father. "All me boys look so handsome tonight." Sidna kissed Riley's cheek and hugged him tightly. "So proud of you, love. So, so proud."

"Thanks, Mam." He kissed the top of her head as Claron Senior stood beside Murphy. Sidna's gaze fell upon Conor and she extended her hands out.

"Oh, me boyo." She cupped his face and kissed him, bringing him into a tight hug. "Did your Mammy get a look at ye?"

"Aye." Conor nodded and received an affectionate look of approval.

Sidna hugged Murphy as she watched Conor's gaze flutter towards the dance floor and to Chloe. Her daughter danced with a handsome lad she didn't know, but Conor's look of disapproval intrigued her. "Seems our Chloe has found her legs."

"Aye," Murphy agreed. "Can't look like that and not expect a few lads to take notice."

"Always a beauty, our Chloe. Who be the man?" Sidna asked.

"Kelly," Riley answered.

"A Kelly?" Senior asked. "From where?"

"Here in Galway."

He let out a low growl of disapproval. "No good comes from the Kellys in Galway."

"I'm sure there are a many, love," Sidna assured him. "He may not be kin to the ones you're thinking of."

"A Kelly is a Kelly, no matter what," Senior continued. "The man be a right chancer, just putting on airs, I'm certain of it."

The music ended and Chloe and Quinn began walking their direction. Chloe's eyes brightened at the sight of her parents.

"A right rumbly shaper, he is," Senior muttered under his breath as Quinn reached them.

Riley eyed his father in interest, and his attention then went to Quinn. He extended his hand. "Riley," Quinn greeted. "Good to see you again, mate. Nice work here."

"Thanks. Glad you could make it."

"Oh aye. Piper insisted I needed to see the space. Glad I came." He eyed Chloe with eyes like a hawk and Riley sensed a bit of Conor's frustration towards the man might be accurate.

"This be my parents. Claron and Sidna."

Quinn tenderly took Sidna's hand and kissed it, his obvious charm working on Chloe's mam. Conor cringed.

Senior stepped forward and firmly gripped the man's hand. "And what Kellys you be kin to, boyo?"

"Alan and Esther," Quinn reported. "Those are my parents. They live—"

"Over near Grace. In the row houses?"

"Aye." Quinn squinted as if he couldn't fathom how Claron O'Rifcan would know his parents.

"I see." He looked to Sidna with a 'told you so' look and then took a long sip of his champagne. "A man will waste away on such a drink. I need a whiskey."

"I'll fetch it," Heidi offered, sensing tension and wanting to escape. "I need to grab me a new drink anyhow."

"That be a fine lass." Senior nodded as she walked off, Riley reluctantly releasing her hand.

"I'm in real estate and have had me eye on this place for some time. Riley slipped under the radar and snatched it." Quinn began. "I've always been a man who gets what he wants, but when it came to this building, Piper told me it was a lost cause."

"No need to talk about yourself while you're here, lad. We'll surely be doin' that after you leave." Senior's harsh treatment had Quinn's shoulders straighten.

Riley and Murphy exchanged a guarded look with one another, and Murphy pointed to the bar. "Let me buy you a pint, Kelly." He nudged Quinn away from his father and towards Piper.

Chloe looked to her father. "And what be that treatment for, Da?"

"You stay away from that lad, Chloe lass. You hear me?"

She brushed a hand over his arm. "I assure you he was kind." She looked to Conor. "Perhaps my first assessment of his character wasn't fair."

"You mean to tell me you've seen the lad before?" Senior's face fell as slight disappointment seeped into his green gaze.

"Only once." Chloe told him the story of him coming to her flat and Senior eyed Conor's reaction to the story.

"Glad you were there, Conor. The Kelly clan... I dislike the lot of'em."

"Why?" Chloe asked.

"They'll sell ya the eye out of your head if you're not careful. Scheming snakes, they are."

"Now dear." Sidna laid a hand on his arm. "Here is not the place. And our little ones are old enough now to make their own judgments."

"I don't like the look of him either," Senior continued, and Chloe and Conor bit back smiles. Not much stirred Claron Senior's temper, and if Quinn Kelly's name created such a fuss, they knew Senior's opinion was worth considering.

"'Twas only a dance, Da," Chloe insisted. "Nothing more. Besides, I was hoping Conor would give me a spin next."

Conor's brows rose and he turned to her. "Me?"

"Aye." She shrugged her shoulders and smiled shyly. "If you'd like, that is?"

Conor, not one to turn down dancing, set his glass down. "Chloe O'Rifcan, there'd be nothing I'd like more."

∞

Chloe floated, a content sigh escaping her lips as she walked over the bricked walkways of Eyre Square and towards her car in the lot a few blocks down. Music drifted through doors to pubs and restaurants, the chatter of friendly conversations and late-night chats warming her. She wasn't much for the city, but in moments like this, where she could listen and hear the life behind it, she could begin to see its charm. Riley's gala had turned into a wonderful night. She'd danced with Conor, not once, but three times, and each time seemed different. The first, in true Conor form, had him stepping all over her feet. The second was a wee bit smoother but slower. And the third, she paused as she sensed someone staring at her. Not seeing anyone, she continued on her way. She'd slipped out when everyone had been distracted, knowing they'd all try to convince her to stay. But it was late, and Chloe had had her fill. Her mother had roped Conor in for a dance while her da was having a pint with Murphy at the bar. And the rest of her siblings were with their loves or dates, simply enjoying a night out. By the time they'd notice her missing, she'd be halfway to Castlebrook and her own comfortable bed.

She felt the breeze rising off the Lough Atalia harbor and turned towards the lot where her car awaited her. She fetched her keys from her handbag and started to unlock her door. She heard footsteps hurry behind her. Turning, her heart leapt in her throat at Quinn Kelly's approach. Breathless, he stopped before her, his breaths carrying the light scent of whiskey. He held a hand to his chest as he panted. He held up a finger with a wide smile so as to catch one last breath. He straightened and stood. "Why the early night, Chloe? I was hoping to steal you for another dance, lass."

"I'm not much of a night owl. I thought I would leave on a high note. Thank you though, for the dance earlier." She smiled politely and unlocked her car. When she reached to open the door, his hand halted her movement. She turned and he stood close, the smell of whiskey and an odd cologne wafting through the air and covering up the soothing scents of the harbor. "Quinn, please. I really would like to leave."

"What is it," he asked curiously, his finger lightly tracing her jawline. "That has a beautiful lass like you runnin' so scared from me? I've never had such a chase." He grinned and took a step back and Chloe visibly relaxed.

"I'm just not interested. You seem nice and all, don't get me wrong, I just... am not wishing for more than a casual dance at the pub."

His eyes hardened a moment and he fisted his hands on his lean hips. "I see. So, a successful businessman from Galway is not good enough for a wee lass from Castlebrook, is he?"

"That's not what I said," she corrected, her voice taking offense. "I just said I'm not interested in... whatever 'tis you're offering."

Baffled, he held his arms out. "And why not?"

"For one, you're challengin' my feelings instead of respectin' them." Her temper flared and her cheeks flushed as she took a step towards him. Her stubborn chin tilted up as she looked him in the eye. "And that right there tells me you're not a man I wish to see, Quinn Kelly. Now go. Enjoy the rest of yer night with friends. I'll save a dance with you next time you're in Castlebrook."

He rubbed his hand down her arm and threaded his fingers through hers. "And what if we didn't go back to the gala at all? What if we just walked the square, slipped in and out of pubs, and made a night of it? Would you be willing to spend time with me then?"

Sighing, frustrated that he would not get the hint, Chloe shook her head. "Sorry, no. I wish to go home." She took a deep breath. "But thank you, again."

Figuring she'd finally gotten through to him, she reached for her car door again. This time, she felt a hand on her shoulder before being whipped around so fast her heels tangled together. Her back pressed against her window but her face was snatched in Quinn's hands. His lips hard against hers. He pulled his mouth away from hers and stared into her face. Smiling, he began lowering his head once more, only slower and gentler. Chloe gripped her handbag and plopped him on the head with it. He pulled back in surprise and then held up his hands in defense as she whipped him again.

"What the—" He took a step back and felt a firm yank on his arm. He swung around in time to feel a fist meet his jaw and then his knees hit the gravel. "Bloody devil, I—"

"I'd stay there if I were you." Conor's voice was hard, and Chloe'd never seen such a ferocious look on her friend's face. "I believe she said she was leaving. Now be on yer way, Kelly."

Quinn stood to his feet, his hand rubbing his bruised jaw that no doubt would show signs of his rude behavior the next morning. He cast Chloe one last look and Conor stepped in his path to block his view. Quinn gave a nod and a small chuckle. "You know... I've never quite had this reaction before. I'll be seeing you, Chloe." He leaned so as to peer behind Conor, and Conor took a step towards the man that had Quinn retreating. He gave one last venomous look at the two of them and hurried back towards the crowded streets. Chloe reached forward and grabbed one of Conor's fists. He jerked but then relaxed when he saw her distressed features.

"Thank you, Conor." His name released on a shaky breath.

"You alright now, Chloe?"

"Aye. I think so. Perfect timing on yer part. Thank you." She stepped towards him and onto her tip toes, her hands shaking as she slid her arms around his neck and gave him a grateful hug. She brushed her lips lightly over his cheek and then sank back to her feet. She then fished for her keys on the ground and her hands shook as she stood.

He cupped her hands in his. "How about I take you home, lass?" He silently removed her keys and walked her towards the passenger side of the car and opened the door. "In you go, now." She watched as he circled the hood of the car and attempted to squeeze his large frame and long legs behind the wheel. He adjusted the seat and cranked the engine and pulled out of the lot headed towards home.

«CHAPTER ELEVEN»

The gala was over, and it was now Conor's responsibility to help plan Claron's stag party and find yet another suit for the wedding. They had a month. A wee month to get their act together, and he wasn't quite sure it would all come together. The women seemed more optimistic. Though he wasn't sure about Chloe. They'd barely spoken since the gala. The ride back to Castlebrook was silent as she stared out the window. He wasn't quite sure what to say to her after the incident with Quinn Kelly. She'd thanked him for driving her home and that was that. He hadn't spoken to her since. It'd been four days and he was about to go crazy. When he arrived at Mam's restaurant, she'd already left. When he buzzed by Sidna's, she was waiting tables. When he walked by her shop, she was out and about gathering prices and quotes for Rhea's flower wish list. She was a busy bee who flew about, easily heard, but hard to catch. And he wasn't quite sure what he'd say to her if he did catch her. All he knew was that something was different between them. Or perhaps it was all in his mind, but he needed to find out either way. *Right?*

He raised his head as he heard his name, and Declan O'Rifcan walked up to him with the usual O'Rifcan swagger of confidence and radiant smile. "Aye there, Conor. Your head in the clouds? Been calling your name for the last two minutes."

"Sorry, lad. A bit distracted." He set his tool bag down as Declan began delighting him with news of his "great find" for Clary's stag party.

"So, I'll bring it and we'll see which stupid one of us takes the first plunge."

"And your wife, the nurse, is okay with this?" Conor asked.

Declan laughed. "Oh, Aine... she doesn't quite know. She'd only shake her head in dismay."

"As she should."

Declan laughed. "Yes, well we'll see who hops up there first once they've had a bit of liquid courage." He thumped Conor on the shoulder as if he nominated him. Conor watched him go and then picked up his tools.

"Crazy O'Rifcans." He muttered on a grin as he walked toward Murphy's Pub. He walked inside and Murphy waved from behind the bar.

"G'day to you Conor. Thanks for coming so quickly." Murphy pointed to two broken chairs resting on a table. "The lads got a bit out of hand last night."

"I hope you charged them extra."

"Of course I did." He grinned. "So, how's your day going?"

"Busy," Conor replied as he started surveying the split wooden legs and bases. He reached into his bag and withdrew some sandpaper. "This be a pretty easy fix. Left me wood glue over at Clary's. I'll fetch it and be back."

"Your lorry up and runnin'?" Murphy asked.

"No, but I'm borrowing your da's 'ol rusty."

"Ah, good. See you in a bit. If I'm not here, have your way with the place." Murphy motioned towards the chairs. "But don't go crazy." He grinned at Conor as Conor made his way to the door.

Conor tossed his bag in the back of the old green lorry and made his way towards Claron's. It was a short drive, and it was in between milkings, so Claron was home. As was Roland and Chloe. The three sat on the back porch overlooking the Gap when Conor interrupted their banter. Roland smiled in greeting. "Conor, good to see you."

"Roland." He nodded. "Chloe." Her cheeks deepened in color as she said hello. "Clary, I left me wood glue at yer barn. Came to fetch it."

"No problem." Claron stood and walked with him down the slope.

"Sorry to interrupt your relaxing time between milkings."

"Don't be. Chloe was discussing flowers for the arch you're building for Rhea. I'm not much for talking of flowers."

"You seem awfully calm for a man who will be married in a few short weeks."

Claron chuckled as he stuffed his hands in his pockets. "Aye. I think I'm just ready to be over and done with it. Not in a bad way, just ready for Rhea to be here all the time."

Conor grinned. "She'll suit these hills just fine, that's for certain."

"Aye. I envision her there on the porch with her cup of tea. I think about it so often I believe I see her there at times. Fairy tricks, I suppose." A bark sounded as Rugby came running from Conor's land that backed up to Claron's barn. The brown ball of fur jumped to lick the men's hands as they walked, and Claron playfully shoved him away.

"'Tis a beautiful vision to think about. I don't blame you for doing so," Conor admitted.

"I also envision that house." He pointed towards Conor's abandoned family home. "I see it blooming with life and family again. You and me tossing a bottle back at the end of the day right here at the barn. Wee ones runnin' back and forth."

"I like that vision as well," Conor told him. "And I'd be lying if I said I didn't want it."

"Sometimes you just have to take the plunge, Conor," Claron told him. "Even if it seems you're not ready. I never would have foreseen my life turning out the way it has. Rhea and... all this." He waved his hand towards the cottage where Roland waved to them as he climbed into his truck to leave. "But when it's meant, it's meant, and you can't stand in the way of fate."

"Aye."

"So you best decide what to do with that house." Claron nodded again towards Conor's land. "Because I aim to buy it from you if you don't."

Conor hooted in laughter at his friend's lack of subtlety. "You sneak." He punched Claron in the arm and then grabbed his wood glue from the bench. "That land is not for sale. Not even to me best mate."

Claron shrugged. "I'll keep being persistent then."

"On with ye now," Conor chuckled. "I'm to head back to Murphy."

"Ah, the pub. The official sunblock of Ireland."

Conor laughed as he nodded. "Seems Murphy had some wildlings last night. A few broken chairs need attention."

"They'll keep for a while longer I imagine." Claron pointed towards Conor's house. "Take a walk."

Claron started walking back to his cottage and Conor watched as he conversed with his sister a moment. Perhaps he could take a few minutes to walk the property. He hadn't taken the time the last month or so, and it did clear his mind each time he did. He also liked to make sure the house was secure, no extra critters taking up residence in his absence. Claron was a good friend, seeing about the house when Conor couldn't. But it was his responsibility, not Claron's, and taking a few minutes to do a walk about wouldn't hurt him.

He cast one last look up the hill and Chloe's red hair danced in the ever-present breeze as she penciled something on a clipboard. No doubt making notes of some of Rhea and Roland's wishes for the arch he'd yet to build. It wouldn't take him long. He'd drafted the sketch and cut the wood. He just needed to assemble and then stain. A few days' work and it would be complete. The breeze carried to him and the grass softly swayed. He brushed his hands over the top of the blades and decided he would sit a spell and enjoy the view of the Gap before heading back to Murphy's.

∞

Chloe finished the notation on her clipboard. Roses, check. Peonies, check. Astilbe, check. Seeded eucalyptus, check. She tapped her pencil against her chin as she looked to the edge of the cliff where the arch would stand. She envisioned the structure in her mind and began sketching it on her notepad. The wind picked up and the papers on her clipboard began to flutter as she tried to finish the last of her drawing. She tucked the pencil in her hair and turned to walk to her car. That's when she spotted him down the hill.

He laid flat on his back in the middle of the green grass, his legs splayed out and arms outstretched. He wasn't moving. She dropped her clipboard and sprinted, yelling over her shoulder for Claron to help her. Panic seized her chest as she frantically hopped the fence separating Conor's property from her brother's. She leapt, swinging her legs over and plopped to the ground and sprinted, running towards Conor's figure. When she neared him, his head slightly turned at her arrival and his eyes widened as her run turned into a slide and she landed beside him with a thump, her hands plopping hard against his chest. He grunted and her eyes adjusted to the fact he was moving. "You alright?" Her hands swept over his face and chest and to his neck to check his pulse. Her bun had come undone and her red hair whipped in the wind.

"What the devil?" Conor attempted to sit up and Chloe shoved him back on the ground. "Chloe, Chloe, Chloe." He swatted her hands away from his face and spotted a tear slide down her cheek as she realized he now held her hands away from him. "What's gotten into you, lass?" He slowly eased up from his back and sat, holding her wrists.

"Conor? You're okay?"

"Of course I'm okay, why would I bloody not be?"

"You were here. I was on the hill." She pointed towards Claron's house, her brother just now stepping out onto the porch. Conor offered him a wave and Claron returned it, venturing back inside the cottage.

"Alright," Conor prodded.

"And you were on your back. I thought... I thought you were... dead or hurt or somethin' worse." She tugged on her hands and he released her wrists. "I—" She then punched him hard in the shoulder. "Don't ever scare me like that again."

Conor's lips twitched until he saw the pure relief in her watery eyes. "Oh now, we don't be needin' that." He lightly ran a finger under her eye and caught a tear, and she bit back another sob. He tenderly pulled her into his chest and rubbed her back, giving small shushing sounds to calm her raw nerves. "I be just fine. Just soaking in the day a bit is all."

"You're a right fool, Conor McCarthy, scaring me like that." She pulled back and looked up at him. "A right fool. Bloody eegjit," she repeated.

He chuckled and hugged her to him again, pleased that she would come to his aid. "I'm glad you would come to me rescue in such a way."

She clung to him. The hearty chest beneath her head held a strong heartbeat and the arms that wrapped around her had strength. And tenderness, she realized. Embarrassed now for overreacting, she pulled from his embrace and swiped her hands over her face erasing the last of her tears. "My heart 'bout left me, seeing you flat on yer back like that." She held a hand to her chest. "Scared me so."

He gently took her hand in his and rubbed his thumb over her knuckles. "I'm sorry for worryin' ya, Chloe."

"Worry me?!" Her voice rose. "Panicked, I was!"

"No need to yell now."

"I'm not yelling!" she defended, her voice clearly rising. "I'm Irish!"

Her comment had them both pause and laughs seeped through and eased the tension. "I'm sorry for hitting you," she apologized, her voice calmer.

"As you should be," he teased.

She grinned and leaned back on her haunches. She surveyed the spot in which he laid. "'Tis a beautiful spot though."

"Aye. One of my favorites."

Her gaze found his again and shyness crept into her cheeks.

"You've been avoiding me as of late, Chloe O'Rifcan. I'm glad you're talking to me now. Though I could have done without the pummel."

"Avoiding you?" Her eyes narrowed. "I haven't been avoiding you."

"Aye, you have. And you know it." He pointed at her and she swatted his finger away. "You know you have nothing to be ashamed or embarrassed of about Galway, right?"

"I know. Though I am."

"And why, lass? Not yer fault Quinn Kelly is a right scoundrel."

She lowered her head and he lifted her chin until she looked at him again. "I mean it, Chloe. Nothing for you to think on anymore. Alright?"

She nodded and he released her chin. "Good."

Chloe watched as he took one last long look at his land. He took a deep breath as if savoring the quiet and the atmosphere. He turned, about to say something, but she didn't let him. Instead, she pressed her lips to his.

Neither of them moved. And as she slowly pulled her lips from his, she rested her forehead against his. Clearing her throat, she closed her eyes to beat back further humiliation for doing such a thing. "I'm sorry, Conor. I just—" His lips were on hers again, eager and soft. And his hands framed her face as her hair slashed through the air and surrounded them. She felt her body lean into his and her heart leapt much like she had over the fence. Her hands rested against Conor's chest as his lips continued to glide over hers. She completely lost herself in his touch and the achingly sweet tenderness in which he kissed her.

A jingle filtered through the air and had Conor pulling back. Both were breathless and their eyes held a mixture of uncertainty and hope. His hand found his phone and he eyed the caller id. Murphy. Chloe closed her eyes. *What was she thinking?* Conor was her brothers' friend. Claron's *best* friend, and she had kissed him. He held up his hand for her not to leave as he answered the phone.

"Murphy," he greeted and listened. "Aye, I was just heading back... Aye, I will see to that as well while I'm there... right... have a care." He hung up, his eyes studying Chloe a moment until he ran a hand over his beard.

"Don't," Chloe told him. "I already know what you're going to say."

"And what is that?" he asked.

"That this shouldn't have happened. I'm sorry. I just—"

He grabbed her hand and kissed the back of it, her words trailing off. "That was not what I was going to say, lass."

"Oh."

He climbed to his feet and helped her to stand as well. "What I will say is that I would like to discuss this..." He motioned between the two of them. "*This.*"

"Conor, I'm not sure we sh—"

"No," he said, his voice confident. "I think we'd be fools not to, Chloe."

"Really?" She looked up at him and he gently brushed his thumb over her soft cheek, the action turning her legs to mush.

His smile sent butterflies to dancing in her stomach. "I have to go now," he said. "But perhaps you will not avoid me, and we could meet for a bite later."

"Perhaps," she replied, causing one of his grins to spread over his face. "But I have to go to Shannon."

"Shannon? Whatever for?"

She smiled at his disappointment. "Flowers for Rhea's bridal portraits. I be picking them up today and placing the final order for the wedding."

"Ah. I see."

"But I could call you when I get back," she added nervously.

He answered with a smack on her lips that had them both laughing giddily as she wrapped her arms around his neck, and he twirled her in a circle.

«CHAPTER TWELVE»

Conor finished Murphy's chairs to the sounds of a quiet bar. It'd be a good hour before people began filtering in for the evening craic they sought after a long day of working. He checked his phone and still no message from Chloe. No matter, he still needed to take Layla her finished stools.

He stepped outside and the sun had slowly begun to sink, turning day into evening. He spotted Layla about to leave her shop and hollered. She turned, her face splitting into a smile at his approach.

"Warms my heart for a man to call out at me. Hadn't realized I missed it until just now."

Conor chuckled. "Well, I'm glad I could fluff the ego a bit, lass."

She smiled. "What can I do for you, Conor?"

"I have your stools."

Her eyes brightened and she clasped her hands together. "Oh, now, that would certainly end my day just fine."

"Come. They be in the back of me lorry." He motioned towards Senior's old pickup and leaned over the side to fetch the first one. When he set it on the ground, Layla gasped.

"Oh, Conor..." She ran her hand over the top and smiled up at him. "The tile is gorgeous. Thank you."

"Is it what you wanted?"

"More than. Certainly more than."

"Good."

"Let me fetch me purse and I will pay you."

He waved it off. "Save it for another day."

"Alright. Where you be headed? Coming to the pub? Most of us will be there."

"I might," he answered, not wanting to reveal his plans to eat with Chloe just yet.

"You should." She lifted a stool and Conor grabbed the other as they set it just inside the door of the shop. She locked the door once more. "You've seriously outdone yourself on those. Chloe will be so jealous." She giggled. "Oh, she was fightin' mad that I asked you to add the tile but look at them. Beautiful. Absolutely stunnin'."

"I'm glad they're to yer liking, Layla lass."

"After you check in with your Mam, because I'm assuming that's where you are headed next," she waited while he nodded. "Come to the pub. Your first pint is on me." She winked as she headed towards her little red sports car and tossed him a final wave as she pulled away from the curb.

Rhea's car pulled into the spot to replace Layla's and she waved as she and Heidi climbed out.

"Is it just me lucky day to keep bumping into beautiful lasses?" He accepted their hugs and Rhea pointed towards the pub. "We're early, but we're headed to Murphy's."

Heidi linked her arm with his and rested her head on his shoulder as they somehow turned his feet towards the pub and had him at the door before he could change his mind. "Devious little faeries, the both of ye."

Rhea smiled. "I just saw your Mam. She was with Sidna and told me if I saw you to let you know she was fine and enjoying her visit, and for you to do the same."

"Simple enough." Conor opened the pub's door for them and Murphy stood behind the bar prepping glasses and refreshing bottles.

"Hello, Rhea darling." Murphy beamed and then he leaned across the bar and winked. "Heidi, me love."

Heidi palmed his face, pushing him back behind the counter and he laughed. "You two little birds are a bit early, but I see you've brought an escort."

"Claron was still in the fields," Rhea reported.

"And Riley's on his way." Heidi sighed as she sat on a stool and plopped her purse on the bar.

"And I'm done for the day," Conor added.

"Well, then it seems you will all be needin' a bit of sustenance." Murphy poured them each a pint and set it before them. He looked up as Jace and Jaron walked inside. "What is it with you two lately?" He asked. "'Tis like Tweedle Dee and Tweedle Dum, always together."

"Don't be snarky," Jaron warned him. "Just because I like Jace better than you doesn't mean I don't love you all the same."

Murphy rolled his eyes as he began pouring two new pints. "Is there a family meetin' I'm not aware of?"

"No," Rhea answered. "We just all wanted to see your face today."

He leaned flirtatiously over the bar and tapped Rhea's hand. "Rhea love, if you're having second thoughts about Clary now..." He winked, knowing full well she wasn't and that he could simply make her blush. He was rewarded with a light pink flush to her cheeks.

"Easy there, brother," Claron's voice called from the doorway, his clothes stained from his day's work, but his eyes and smile were only for Rhea. She straightened at his entrance and her face gleamed in love when he walked towards her. He kissed her, until the room fell silent.

"Now that is a nice finish to a long day," Heidi pointed out. "Riley better get here quick."

Murphy started to speak, and Heidi held up a finger. "Don't *even* offer yourself, Murphy O'Rifcan." He laughed and held a hand to his heart as if she wounded him.

His face sobered immediately as his pub door crashed open, bouncing off the wall behind it and Riley stormed inside, eyes wild.

Heidi hopped to her feet, concern etched on forehead as she walked towards him. He looked to all of them. "Where be Tommy?"

"Workin' still, I imagine," Murphy supplied. "What's the problem, brother?"

Everyone's nerves became unsettled as Riley's tormented eyes looked to all of them. "Chloe."

Conor stood so quickly his stool knocked over. "What about her?" he asked.

"Declan called. She had an accident."

Conor was halfway across the room and walking towards the door. Riley grabbed his arm. "Shannon hospital."

Everyone scrambled and Murphy hopped the bar and grabbed his car keys.

"How bad?" Rhea asked in a panic.

"Not good. Mam and Da are already on their way. As is Roland. I was to fetch you all. I'll call Tommy on our way." He reached for Heidi's hand as he pulled her towards the door.

Conor climbed into Claron's truck with him and Rhea as they watched Murphy flip the sign on his door. There would be no fun night at the pub. Not for them or for anyone. Conor's heart pounded in his chest, and he prayed Chloe wasn't hurt. That perhaps it wasn't her little car after all. Not having any details on the accident only made his fear worse. He sat silently as Claron and Rhea tossed about theories and concern. He didn't want to think about what shape Chloe might be in. All he wanted was to see her for himself. To go back to this afternoon when they'd shared their feelings for one another with the promise of more... or at least a talk of potentially having more.

The drive seemed to take forever, but Conor peered over Claron's shoulder and noticed him driving over the speed limit. Riley's truck was ahead of them containing Riley, Heidi, Jaron, and Jace. Murphy brought up the rear behind Clary. A red sports car flew past all of them as Layla must have been called and was panicked over her sister.

"She best take it slow or Chloe won't be the only one in an accident," Claron muttered.

"She's probably terrified," Rhea defended. "As we all are."

They reached the hospital all in record time and all rushed through the sliding doors of the emergency room entrance. Riley headed towards the counter to ask the attending nurse where Chloe was located. No sin of their parents told them she'd already been moved somewhere in the vast hospital.

Riley turned. "This way," he told them. In unison, they all marched the halls and headed towards the elevator, heads turning at such a large group moving together. Riley pressed the three and the doors closed. Conor tried to squeeze further back into the corner to make more room, but the O'Rifcan men were all tall and broad like their father, so space was limited.

When the doors opened, Jace began walking towards the waiting room and everyone followed. Sidna and Senior stood at their entry. Jeanie, Doireean, and Roland did as well as hugs were exchanged. Conor's mother met him halfway and hugged him close before he walked towards Sidna and Senior. "What's the word?" he asked.

"She be in surgery." Sidna wound her hands together nervously and Senior reached over and took them in his own.

"She be in good hands, love. Aine is with her."

"What happened?" Rhea asked, her arm draped over her grandpa's shoulders as her mother held her around the waist.

"Declan says she was headed back to Castlebrook when a lorry swerved in her lane. She tried to dodge it and careened out of her lane... hitting another lorry head on."

Conor felt his knees go weak as the women gasped and the brothers' faces paled.

"Head on?" Clary's voice was soft as the gravity of the crash had them all desperately clinging to one another. Conor felt Layla's nails digging into his arm as she waited for more information.

"Aye." Declan turned at the sound of footfalls as Aine walked towards them. The O'Rifcans swarmedaround her with a million questions. She held up her hand, her face tired, and a little sad.

"She's out of surgery," she announced. "Still knocked out but should be coming around in the next half hour. She was lucky." Aine continued. "She has a severely broken leg, which was what the surgery was for. She now has two rods in her right leg. Her knee was preserved, somehow." Aine looked baffled. "She has some stitching on her arms and forehead from glass and hitting the steering wheel. Seems she curved enough that her face did not hit full impact. Probably saved her life. She has a concussion and some bruised ribs, but other than the leg, nothing is broken."

Sidna's grateful sob broke through and Senior pulled her close.

"When can we see her?" Conor asked, his question surprising the siblings.

"Not until she wakes up, and even then, not all at once," Aine answered. "I'll let you know when she's awake." Declan gave her a reassuring hug as she hurried back down the hall.

Drained from their hurried road trip, the O'Rifcans sat amongst the waiting room. A clipped sound of polished shoes on tile hurried towards them as Delaney appeared, his eyes immediately seeking out an upset Layla. He pulled her into his arms and whispered something to her as Tommy, the last O'Rifcan brother entered and sat by his mother. He nodded to assure the brothers that he knew the extent of Chloe's situation. Conor felt Rhea's hand slide into his as she sat between he and Clary. Her other hand resting in Claron's. Conor stared at the clock and watched the hands tick by as his mind continued to flashback to her beautiful and timid smile in his meadow earlier that day. *How quickly a day and a life could change*, he thought. *How dim they could seem when a bright and warm person like Chloe could be taken from them.* He hated the thought. He hated the way his heart reacted at the thought of losing her. And he hated that he was stuck in the waiting room watching the time keep ticking away. Sighing, he lowered his forehead into his free hand and prayed.

∞

Chloe blinked. Her head pounded and when she opened her eyes a bright light shined down on her. She tried to turn her head, but she wore a thick neck brace and the movement caused an ache between her shoulder blades. She realized then that her hand was connected to an IV and her leg was elevated by a pulley system, a bright white cast wrapped around it. She closed her eyes and swallowed, her throat dry and her mind swimming.

She tried to focus and remember what had happened. She was driving home, flowers in the back seat of her car. She thought of Conor and their kiss and remembered the excitement she felt heading back to Castlebrook to talk with him about what had seemed to develop between them. That was when the truck next to her swerved into her lane and the lights of the oncoming vehicle blinding her as she attempted to move out its way. She felt the hit all over again. The way her body jerked, the steering wheel crushing into her lungs. The sound of metal scraping against metal, squealing tires, and her screams. The smell of rubber, gasoline, blood, and oddly... flower petals raining down around her. She remembered nothing after that except her brother Declan's face floating before her. *Had he found her? Or had he been one of the first Guarda on the scene?*

The door to her room opened and Aine stepped inside with a man in a white coat. Her sister in law reached for her hand and squeezed. "Good to see you awake, love."

"I—" Her voice was scratchy and Aine immediately reached for a cup with a straw and held it to Chloe's lips. She drank greedily and then leaned her head back against the firm pillow. "I feel awful."

"As you should, Ms. O'Rifcan," the doctor told her. "You took quite a beating." He explained her injuries and how lucky she was to be alive. She knew that already, but she let him talk, her head aching. "We have you on some pain medication for now. You need rest." The doctor looked at Aine and she smiled begrudgingly.

"The family is here to see you," she told Chloe. "All of them. I already warned them that they couldn't all come in at once. If you do not wish to see anyone, that's understandable for now. But if you'd like, someone could stay with you. Up to you."

"Mam and Da. I'd like to see them." Chloe's eyes felt swollen as she blinked. "Mammy will be worried."

"Aye. They all are." Aine looked to the doctor and nodded that she would see to Chloe and he left. "I'll fetch Sidna and Senior for you."

Chloe nodded and rested her eyes until she heard the door to the room open again. She slightly turned her head and saw her mother standing with her hand over her mouth as she soaked in Chloe's image.

"How's me little gingernut?" her father asked.

She tried to smile but was sure it looked haggard. "I've been better, Da."

"Gave us a fright, you did." He stepped forward, his looming presence a comfort as he tenderly rubbed his knuckle over her bruised cheek. "Doc says you'll be laid up for a bit."

"Aye. I can see that."

He smirked. "Told 'im nothing could keep ye down for long."

She reached for his hand and he gripped hers tight as if his fear of losing her would be realized if he let go. Sidna stepped forward finally and she brushed Chloe's hair aside and off her forehead. "Me little one," she blubbered. "We were all so scared. I'm so happy you're awake."

Chloe's eyes watered as her mother kissed her forehead. "You need anythin'? A blanket? Some water?" She reached for the cup and Chloe shook her head. Disappointed that she couldn't tend to her, Sidna set the cup down and twiddled her hands together before lightly placing them on Chloe's arm.

"Aine said everyone was waiting to see me."

"Aye. Every last one," Sidna confirmed. "Your brothers and Layla. Lorena's just arrived with the kids. She had to shut down the café for me. Roland and Jeanie are here of course. Delaney. Conor and Doireean."

"Conor be here?" she asked.

"Aye. Right sick, he is."

"I'd like to see him first."

Sidna's brows rose at her daughter's request.

"Alright, dearie."

Senior walked out of the room and moments later he emerged, a hesitant Conor behind him. Conor's face blanched when he saw her and she couldn't imagine what he saw. He rushed to her side and knelt beside her, his hand tenderly resting on top of her curls. He kissed the back of her hand. Her parents exchanged a look of curiosity but said nothing. She smiled, knowing it was an incredible accomplishment to make Sidna O'Rifcan speechless.

"Hey there, Coppertop," Conor whispered.

Chloe stared into his sweet gaze and a tear slipped from her eye and down the side of her temple. He gently swiped it away. "I'm sorry I didn't call."

He choked on a laugh as he pulled a nearby rolling stool towards the bed and sat, leaning on the edge so as not to break their connection. "Hurt my feelings, you did. Ignorin' me and all."

She tried to grin as he stared down at her leg. "Seems you'll be a bit off-center for a wee bit."

"Just a bit. Hope Rhea doesn't mind a hobbling bridesmaid."

"I'll carry you," he said, and she chuckled, the movement sending sharp pains through her achy ribs.

"Stop making me laugh. It hurts."

Concern etched his face and she removed her hand from his so as to brush the back of her hand over his beard. "Will you come tomorrow?"

"Aye. I'm not leavin'," he assured her. "I'll be right outside the whole night, if you need me."

"I'd like that."

"Perhaps we'll get that bite after all... just a little later than intended. And it's probably just going to be pudding." He squeezed her hand and kissed it again. "Rest now, lass."

Her eyes were already growing heavy when he stood and placed her hand under the blanket to stay warm.

"She's a strong one," Sidna stated proudly.

"Aye. The strongest," Conor agreed, turning to face her parents.

Senior stepped towards him and placed a hand on his shoulder, his green gaze so similar to Clary's it was almost unnerving. "You're a good man, Conor McCarthy, always have been. I count you as one of me own."

Chloe peeked through half-opened lids and her mother caught her stare. Sidna winked at her. Clearly her mother was thrilled at what she just saw between Conor and herself. And that was a pleasing thought.

"We'll fetch ye once her brothers have seen her," Senior continued.

"Thank you." Conor shook his hand. He looked at Chloe one more time before walking back out into the waiting room.

∞

"I'm a bit tired of pudding," Chloe whined as Conor walked in carrying two cups from the hospital cafeteria.

He grinned. "Aye, me too. But it's the snack they have, and Aine was watching me. Otherwise, I would have snuck you some crisps."

Chloe smiled and shifted against her pillows to sit up straighter. Today was to be her final morning in the hospital, and Conor had driven to Shannon to pick her up. They were just waiting on the all clear from the doctor and then he could carry her home.

"Your mammy called to see if we were on the way," he told her. "Not yet, I said, as we're still waiting."

Chloe took a bite of her pudding. "And the first thing we are going to do is grab a bite to eat on the way home. I be tired of this food. And I'm starving."

"I'm glad to see your appetite is back."

"Well, I've been here four days, it best be. Thanks for coming to see me every day. I know 'tis not convenient driving so far, but—"

He reached over and swallowed her small hand in his own. "Chloe O'Rifcan, you best be prepared for me never letting you out of me sight again."

A sweet smile spread over her face. "That so?"

"Aye. If you wish it as well." He held his breath as he waited for her to reply.

"I've always enjoyed your company, Conor."

Her answer deflated him a bit, realizing he was slowly slipping back into friend zone, but he forced a smile.

To his relief, she continued. "But I think I've grown to love it."

He raised his eyes back to hers and let out a happy yell that made her laugh and then cringe as she placed a hand to her ribs. He gently cupped her face and kissed her. "That be the way of it then, Chloe O'Rifcan. That be the way."

The door opened and Aine and the doctor walked inside, Aine's brows rising into her hairline at the sight of them intimately close. Though she'd no doubt come to suspect Conor's feelings for Chloe, as most of the O'Rifcans probably did, none had witnessed or even asked. Yet.

"Well, Ms. O'Rifcan, it would seem this is the last of our time together." The doctor smiled as he handed her a clipboard for her to sign while talking of limitations and when she'd need to come back for checkup appointments. Chloe nodded and then looked to Aine.

"May I shower before leaving? I feel somewhat gross, not having really been out of this bed for days."

"Aye. I'll help you." Aine nudged Conor to roll his stool out of the way as she helped Chloe swing her casted leg over the side of the bed and handed her crutches. Her arms were still weak, but she managed to shakily make her way towards the bath.

"I'll wait outside," Conor called after them. He shook the doctor's hand. "Thank you for seeing to her so well. We all appreciate it."

"It was my pleasure. The O'Rifcans are a grand bunch. This is not me first round with them all." He grinned. "A bit of an intimidating clan if you didn't know them."

"Aye. For certain." Conor chuckled and followed the doctor out into the hall. He waited patiently for another half hour as Aine helped Chloe shower and dress. When the door opened, Chloe sat in a wheel chair, her leg extended out in front of her. Her curls were damp, but her face was freshly scrubbed and she looked relaxed.

"I'm ready to escape now."

He grinned, taking the handles of the wheelchair from Aine. Aine bent down and kissed Chloe's cheek and then kissed Conor's. "You two be careful. I'll be seeing you this evening, Chloe."

Chloe nodded and then sighed happily as they rolled into the elevator and made their way to the parking garage. Conor stopped her in front of a new grey truck.

"What's this?"

"This be my new lorry." He opened the passenger door and then bent down to help her rise to her feet. He may have pulled her closer to him than was necessary, but just the feel of Chloe in his arms reassured him that she was indeed okay. She didn't seem to mind as she rested her head briefly against his chest.

"What made you decide to buy a new one? I thought you were saving to fix your family's property?"

"Oh, I still am," he assured her. "But first I needed a reliable vehicle."

"Guess I'll be needing to look into that soon as well. Well, once I can drive again." She motioned to her leg.

He brushed a hand over her damp hair before lifting her onto the seat. She weighed barely anything, and he could feel her tiredness as her arms dropped into her lap and she leaned her head back against the head rest. Her bruises were still vibrant against her pale skin. Her forehead stitched on the left side. Conor brushed his fingertip over her cheek and her head turned to face him, a tired smile crossing her face. "Rest a bit, love," he told her. "I'll get ye home." And her eyes slowly closed.

∞

She'd never been happier to see Castlebrook's familiar streets and shops. She was even happier when Conor pulled his truck to a stop in front of her mother's B&B. Mam and Da waited on the front steps, waving as Conor hopped out and helped Chloe to the ground. He then fetched her crutches. "Up for it?" he asked.

"I think so."

"You tell me when you're not," he told her.

She nodded and gripped the crutches tightly as she slowly made her way up the entry walkway. "Does a Mammy's heart good to see her little bird up and about. Yes, it does." She kissed Chloe's cheek.

Conor helped lift her onto the stoop and she continued to hobble her way inside. Cheers erupted as her siblings and their significant others scattered about the cramped and cozy sitting room. Rhea draped her arms around her shoulders in a hug and then stepped back so others could do the same. Claron stepped forward and held her chin in his thumb and forefinger. He angled her face this way and that before grinning. "You'll do."

She laughed as he kissed her on the cheek before moving towards Rhea and allowing Riley to step up. One by one everyone greeted her and showed her just a wee bit more attention than was necessary. She loved it. But her arms were growing tired. She cast a look towards Conor, whose gaze had never left her. She found it comforting, and he moved towards her as if he read her silent plea. He led her to the couch and took her crutches and set them aside and then helped ease her down into a sitting position on the couch, her leg extended and resting on the small table in front of it.

"Drink, little sister?" Murphy asked, holding out a glass of lemonade. She took it and drank greedily, the sweet and tart taste hitting her empty stomach in a cold rush. Her stomach grumbled.

"I wasn't just being stubborn," Conor told her. "I was under strict orders from your mam not to feed you so that she could prepare a feast."

"That he was." Sidna slapped him on the back as she walked up to them. "And feast is what we'll do.

All in here so Chloe does not have to move. Lorena dear, let's open the lids."

Sidna had set up a self-serve buffet along her check-in counter and waved for Conor to fix Chloe and himself a plate. "What all would you like?" He looked to Chloe.

"Everything," she told him, and rested her head back against the cushion. He fixed her a plate and brought it to her, sitting next to her. She reached over and slid her hand in his as they waited for others to prepare their meals. The brothers all looked to one another and nodded towards the contact between their old friend and youngest sister. Claron beamed as he pulled Rhea a touch closer and enjoyed his own love.

Heidi noticed and paused. "Whoa." Her voice caused everyone to look at her. They followed her gaze and Sidna's eyes gleamed at the prospect of Conor and Chloe.

"So is this a new thing?" Heidi motioned between the two of them and had them both turning crimson. Conor looked to Chloe as to how she'd like to handle the situation. Instead of answering Heidi, Chloe leaned towards him and kissed him sweetly on the lips. "Aye. A grand new thing."

Sidna shouted in joy as she wrapped her arms around Senior and bounced in excitement. Everyone laughed at her antics and Chloe watched as all her brothers seemed to process the idea of their childhood friend and sister in a relationship. Riley gave her a wink of encouragement, and peace and happiness settled around her heart. Conor had always been a part of their family, it was only right that perhaps sooner than later, he officially would be.

Continue the story with...

Book Five of
The Siblings O'Rifcan Series

All Books in
The Siblings O'Rifcan Series:
Claron
Riley
Layla
Chloe
Murphy

**All titles by Katharine E. Hamilton
Available on Amazon and Amazon Kindle**

Adult Fiction:

The Unfading Lands Series
The Unfading Lands, Part One
Darkness Divided, Part Two
Redemption Rising, Part Three

The Lighthearted Collection
Chicago's Best
Montgomery House
Beautiful Fury

Children's Literature:
The Adventurous Life of Laura Bell
Susie At Your Service
Sissy and Kat

Short Stories:
If the Shoe Fits

Find out more about Katharine and her works at:
www.katharinehamilton.com

Social Media is a great way to connect with Katharine. Check her out on the following:

Facebook: Katharine E. Hamilton
https://www.facebook.com/Katharine-E-Hamilton-282475125097433/

Twitter: @AuthorKatharine
Instagram: @AuthorKatharine

Contact Katharine:
khamiltonauthor@gmail.com

ABOUT THE AUTHOR

Katharine E. Hamilton began writing a decade ago by introducing children to three fun stories based on family and friends in her own life. Though she enjoyed writing for children, Katharine moved into adult fiction in 2015 with the release of her first novel, The Unfading Lands, a clean, epic fantasy that landed in Amazon's Hot 100 New Releases on its fourth day of publication and reached #72 in the Top 100 Bestsellers on all of Amazon in its first week. The series did not stop there and the following two books in The Unfading Lands series released in late 2015 and early 2016.

Though comfortable in the fantasy genre, Katharine decided to venture into romance in 2017 and released the first novel in a collection of sweet, clean romances: The Lighthearted Collection. The collection's works would go on to reach bestseller statuses and win Reader's Choice Awards and various Indie Book Awards in 2017 and early 2018.

Katharine has contributed to charitable Indie anthologies and helped other aspiring writers journey their way through the publication process. She loves everything to do with writing and loves that she can continue to share heartwarming stories to a wide array of readers.

She was born and raised in the state of Texas, where she currently resides on a ranch in the heart of brush country with her husband, Brad, and their son, Everett, and their two furry friends, Tulip and Cash. She is a graduate of Texas A&M University, where she received a Bachelor's degree in History.

She is thankful to her readers for allowing her the privilege to turn her dreams into a new adventure for us all.

CPSIA information can be obtained
at www.ICGtesting.com
Printed in the USA
LVHW100753020622
720261LV00002B/258

9 780578 452982